ROUNDABOUT
RANSOM

ROUND
RANSO

Written and illustrated by
PHYLLIS COTÉ

Houghton Mifflin Company Boston 1973

Library of Congress Cataloging in Publication Data

Coté, Phyllis N   1921-
    Roundabout ransom.

    SUMMARY: Ten-year-old Neil is involved in an
unusual adventure after the bully, Trigger, forces him
to hide a suspicious box in his family's toolshed.
    (1. Mystery stories)   I. Title.
PZ7.C827Ro   (Fic)   73-6673
ISBN 0-395-17702-2

CONTENTS

1 Trigger Trouble   1

2 A Tough Bargain   21

3 Noises in the Night   39

4 Free Gym Mats   55

5 Sarsaparilla   75

6 Return Trip   92

7 The Ransom by Mistake   109

8 Joe-Pye Weed   130

for

William Dennis McCarty

with love from
Lornee

Meredith · Dennis · Michael · Peter · Christopher

ROUNDABOUT
RANSOM

1

Trigger Trouble

Y{ou're gonna get me} that key, you little squirt," Trigger Deal said, "or I'll twist your arm off."

Neil gritted his teeth and whacked his heel as hard as he could on Trigger's foot.

Trigger hopped, and howled, and shot a punch at Neil that sent him sprawling to the ground. As Neil rolled over to get up, Trigger sat on him and said, "Now you ready to do what you're told?"

"You big jerk," Neil mumbled, his mouth full of grass.

"Come again?" Trigger said, turning Neil's head by yanking his ear. "Let's get one thing straight. I don't want any trouble from a nosey little nobody like you. If that toolshed door hadn't been locked, I'da been outa your yard before you got home. And you'da been none the wiser. I gotta have the key to that lock and you're gonna get it for me. You're in on this now, kid, right up to your eyeballs, and you'd better believe it."

"You're squashing me," Neil managed to say. "For Pete's sake, at least let me sit up."

"O.K." Trigger said, easing off. Neil hauled himself up and hugged his knees hard to keep from toppling over. His spine felt cracked in two. Trigger anchored him to the spot by ramming his elbows into Neil's ribs.

"Guess this looks better, anyhow," Trigger decided, straightening out his red windbreaker. "You and me just sitting on the grass, having a friendly chat. In case whoever that is coming outa your house right now looks over in this direction."

Both boys glanced up the hill at the Applewhites' house, a sprawling silhouette in the November dusk. In the circle of the back porch light, they could see a woman with a package under her arm crossing to the steps. Halfway down, she turned to say something to Neil's mother who stood in the doorway. (Keep talking! Neil urged her silently. Keep talking till Trigger gets sick of sitting here and goes home.) With a wave of her gloved hand, the woman turned and continued down the steps. They watched her climb into her car which was parked in the driveway and back out of sight. The porch light went out. The air was chilled by an oncoming frost, and Neil shivered in spite of himself.

"Good riddance," Trigger said. "Now here's the pitch. I've got something that's worth a lot of dough. It's in a big box and I'm gonna hide that box in your old man's toolshed. And you're not gonna tell."

Neil had already spotted the box where Trigger had left it over by the lilac bushes. It was a huge corrugated carton with a green label on the side and a layer of newspapers covering the top. Trigger kept a nervous eye on it as he spoke.

"So you helped yourself to some fancy groceries," Neil shrugged. "What's so great about that?" Trigger, an overgrown seventh-grader had an afternoon job as delivery boy for Potter's Market. Elderly Mr. Pike drove the truck and read his paper while Trigger lugged the groceries into the kitchens of their customers. Usually he didn't waste his time on a fourth-grader like Neil. That box of his must have been the largest size Potter's Market used.

"Groceries, my foot!" Trigger snorted. "I told you that box was worth plenty of dough — and that's why I gotta be so careful with it."

"Then hide it at your house," Neil said.

"Not on *my* property, bonehead. I'm not gonna get caught. If anybody hears about this — and I don't care how — I'm gonna say *you* put the box in *your* toolshed. That's one of the best parts of my plan. That and not having a dog around to bark its head off at me every time I show up. Fact is, when I heard your dog got killed by a car the other day, that's when I decided *your* shed would be the best hiding spot in town. No dumb dog to wreck up my plan."

"You shut up about Gypsy."

"Just giving you a sample of my good luck. And it's gonna get better, thanks to little old you."

"I don't get it."

"All you have to get is that key to the lock. Where is it?" Trigger's knuckles jabbed at Neil's jaw. "Next time you'll really feel it. Now where's that key?"

"Hanging on a nail in the garage. Get off me, you big moose. I can't get the key if I'm stuck here, can I?" Neil knew when he was licked.

Trigger allowed Neil to stagger to his feet. "I'm coming with you."

"I told you I'd get it." He stared at Trigger without blinking. He didn't budge.

"Well, step on it," Trigger said finally. "And no funny stuff."

Neil took his time. With a careless flip he tossed the key to Trigger who had to grapple for it.

"You little stinkweed," Trigger muttered. He lurched toward Neil and shoved him over to the toolshed that was attached to the side of the Applewhites' barn which they used for a garage. There were four dusty window panes in the upper half of the panelled shed door. Trigger rattled the key in the lock and turned it noisily. He opened the door with a kick and peered into the darkness. The hulking shapes of stored garden equipment, tools, barrels, and piled up summer furniture half-filled the storage space. There was plenty of room for his box.

"Made to order," Trigger said. "I knew it would be." Without warning he pushed Neil into the toolshed, knocking him off his feet, and slammed the door. *Rattle-Clunkety-Click!* Neil was locked in. Sitting on the cement floor, he rubbed his back where it hurt and turned up his collar. This place was cold as a cellar and dark as a closet. What was that skunk Trigger up to now? Scrambling to the door, Neil climbed up on the picnic table bench and spit on a top clouded window pane, rubbing away the dirt with the sleeve of his jacket. He squinted through the glass and saw Trigger coming forward with the big grocery box in his arms. He was moving slowly and carrying it as carefully balanced as a trayful of teetering glasses.

Whatever's inside, Neil thought, it must be plenty valuable, all right, or Trigger wouldn't be going to so much trouble. And whatever it is, I'm stuck with it. A pushover, that's me. A pushover. He clenched his fists and pounded on the door. "Let me out!" he yelled. "You let me out of here!"

"Clam up," Trigger growled. He set the box down and leaned against the door. "I'll let you out when I'm good and ready. Right now, you listen to me. After you do get out, you stay away from this toolshed like there was a bomb inside. I'm coming back every single day that box is in there, but you'll never know exactly when. If you're lucky, the box won't be there long."

"Suppose my father wants to get something in the toolshed and finds out the key is missing?" This wasn't likely to happen so late in the fall, but the idea might jolt Trigger's plan.

"Your problem. Anyway, he won't be asking *me*

about it. Smarten up, stinkweed. You keep your mouth shut. Don't tell your fat friend Fish — or anyone else — if you want to stay healthy. I got a lot at stake here and if anything goes haywire, you're the one that's on the spot."

"Don't worry," Neil said grimly.

"On a countdown of three, I'll let you out. And you split. Head for the back porch and don't look back."

"O.K., O.K.," Neil said, pressing against the door. "I don't need any more instructions."

"Three — two — " *Rattle-Clunkety-Click!* "One!" The door swung open. Neil pitched out. He flung his arm into Trigger's face as hard as he could and ran off. Trigger's squawk of surprise made Neil's feet pound harder as he raced across the yard to the safety of the back steps. Panting hard, he hung over the porch railing to catch his breath. It was too dark to make out clearly what Trigger was doing at the toolshed. But it didn't matter now, there was nothing Neil could do to stop him. I'm sunk, he thought. Too skinny and no muscles. Well, it won't happen again, not if I can help it. He stood up straight and banged the side of his head with his fist. Only what can I do about it? Suddenly he thought of Fish and an idea Fish had last month. A lifesaver! He had to call Fish right away.

"Hi, Mom. I'm home," Neil called into the kitchen as he tossed his jacket in the direction of a hook in the back hall. "Hello, dear. Hang up your jacket." Mother had heard it plop to the floor. "Dinner will be on the late side tonight. Mrs. Wyman was here to pick up her luncheon cloth and she just left a little while ago. Now she wants me to weave a dozen napkins to match — isn't that nice?"

"Sure is."

"We'll eat in about half an hour. So be washed and ready. Have a good time out playing?"

"Yeah," Neil said. "Great." He raced up the stairs two at a time, heading for the telephone in the hall. "Oh no!" he groaned.

His sister Bonnie was glued to the telephone, the wire draped around her tie-dyed jeans as though it had grown there like a vine. "The shirt has sort of zebra stripes," she was saying. "Yellow and orange with long sleeves."

"Psst! Hurry up," Neil whispered.

Bonnie brushed back her mane of sun-streaked hair, glanced at him through half-closed eyes and shook her

head. "Can't," she whispered. She was almost twelve and she talked a lot.

"It's urgent," Neil said, hopping on one foot and then the other. "Matter of life or death!"

"Ssh," Bonnie said, waving him away as she turned her back. "Oh, Janie, not a poncho with fringe all around!"

In desperation Neil said, "You hang up in five minutes, Bonnie Applewhite, or I'll play your guitar."

"You wouldn't!" she hissed.

"That's what you think," he said, marching down the hall with his wrist watch up to his eyes. "Five minutes."

He went to his room and began to tear through the cubbyholes in his desk. It must be here somewhere, he thought, I know I put it in a safe place. He tossed aside baseball cards, gum wrappers and old snapshots. No good. On the cluttered card table by the window where his ship model, the *Mayflower*, stood half-finished amid an accumulated litter of paint jars, brushes, string, and sandpaper, he hunted still further. He found a horseshoe magnet he had lost and a box of coughdrops. Also the button to his best suitcoat. At last, in the drawer of his bedside table, he pounced on the battered white envelope. It looked fat, and official, and full of importance. He breathed a sigh of relief. Here was his lifesaver if there ever was one.

"Five minutes are up, Bonnie. Right to the dot."

"So soon? Oh, well. I've got to hang up, Janie. Call you back later. Bye." She disentangled herself while grumbling about some people's brothers who don't let them even finish a normal conv sation. "But never mind," she said as she went d stairs. "It's time for me to set the table, anyhow."

Neil put the warm telephone to his ear and dialed Fish's number. Mr. Fisher answered and Neil asked in a rush of words if he could please talk to Fish right away, if they weren't eating or busy or anything, because it was about a very important matter. "In that case," came Mr. Fisher's measured tones, "I will call Barton to the telephone at once. He is eating his second helping of pumpkin pie and could only be disturbed for a reason that sounds as urgent as yours. Hold on, son."

"Thanks, Mr. Fisher," Neil said, hoping he would hurry. With his free hand, he opened the bulky envelope and spread out the enclosed papers on the telephone table. Glancing over them, they were even better than he remembered.

"Hi, Neil," Fish said, after swallowing a couple of times. "What's up?"

"I just got a good idea," Neil said. "Remember those letters we got last month? About Judo lessons?"

"Sure do. I wanted to take and you didn't. On account of football practice. Why?"

"Because I've been thinking it over," Neil said.

"And now I think Judo is much more important than some old sport you just *play*. Judo would help you in your *life* — like if you got held up or something. You could overpower anybody, no matter how much bigger they were. And, boy, that's important."

"You bet it is," Fish agreed. "Do you still have the stuff about it?"

"Right here," Neil said, crackling the papers. They had been sent from the Salisbury YMCA (Youth Department) and were mimeographed in purple.

"Read it to me," Fish said, pleased that he was the one who wanted to sign up in the first place. "I kinda forget what it said."

"O.K.," Neil said. "On the first page, up top, in big letters, it says, 'JOIN THE BEGINNERS' JUDO CLASS.' Then under that it says:

A safe sport for your fun and benefit
Playing techniques explained and demonstrated
Basic principles of balance, position and timing
Roll-outs — Stop-falls — Mat-work
Taught by our expert instructor Dick Grodin — Ex-
   Marine — Brown Belt
Class limited to 10 boys

Starts November 20, Saturday, at 10:00 A.M.
Deadline for registrations: November 15
FILL OUT YOUR APPLICATION NOW."

"We'd better sign up pronto," Fish said. "The fifteenth's next Monday, I know 'cause that's my brother's birthday."

"The sooner the better," Neil said. "Hey, remember the next page? It has some drawings with labels. 'Judo Uniform or *gi* in Japanese (pronounced gee): top, pants and white belt. Order in proper size in time for first class. No other equipment necessary.' "

"Got it," Fish said. "No sneakers or shoes either, 'cause Judo is always barefoot. I know that much."

"Right," Neil said. "And the last thing is the registration card. Do you still have yours?"

"Sure do. All filled out from last time."

"Will your father sign it for you? At the bottom it says, 'Signature of parent.' "

"Course he will. He wanted me to take Judo. But I wouldn't go alone, for gosh sakes. Will your father?"

"He's *got* to. I'll ask him tonight. We can talk about it some more at school."

"O.K., Neil. That's keen. See you tomorrow."

14

"Thanks a lot, Fish. See you."

So far, so good. Neil washed his hands for dinner with a swirl of soapsuds. He stood on tiptoe to look taller in the mirror and slicked down his raggedy brown hair with dripping palms. His big ears gave him some satisfaction ("You'll grow into them," his father had said. "Big ears are a sign of generosity," his mother had said. "You'll be a big man, someday.") His front teeth were pretty big, too. He squinted his blue eyes and jutted out his chin. He made a muscle in his arm and studied the bulge. Same as yesterday. Oh well, all the better to fool you! he half-grinned. Who'd ever guess this joker in the mirror is a Master of Self-Defense, a genuine Judo Champion! Well, not yet he wasn't, but he fully intended to become one. Then nobody'd *dare* call him stinkweed or push him around on his own property. You could bet on that.

When Neil went into the dining room, he was surprised to see there wasn't a place set for his father. "Where's Dad?" he asked.

"He's at a dinner meeting in Salisbury," Bonnie said. "With some other architects." Salisbury, the nearest city, was twenty miles away.

"I bet he doesn't have carrots," Jamie said, wrinkling

his nose. He was six and now that he could read, he especially liked to read menus when he ate in restaurants, which wasn't often. It was the only way he could be sure of never getting carrots or cauliflower to eat.

"When's Dad coming home?" Neil asked anxiously, as he sat down next to Bonnie. Mother placed a steaming tureen of lamb stew (with carrots) on the table and started to ladle it into their bowls.

"Probably not till after midnight," Mother said. "He expects a long session with plenty of discussion. The main speaker is an authority on environment and his subject is 'No More Ivory Towers.' You'll be sound asleep by the time Dad gets here."

"Darn it all. I've got to talk to him about something. Guess it'll have to wait till morning."

"You'll have plenty of time then. Tell me, do you have much homework?"

"Tons," Neil groaned.

"Just heaps," Bonnie sighed.

"None!" Jamie laughed, banging his spoon on his plate. That helped to make up for the carrots.

At night Neil had trouble going to sleep. He missed the warm weight of Gypsy at the foot of his bed. To

16

stop thinking about that, he tried to guess what was in Trigger's big box which was worth "plenty of dough." Maybe it was full of gold or silver or jewels. No, too heavy. What about stacks and stacks of money? On TV paper money from banks was done up in solid packs, like bricks, but you wouldn't need a box that size, even for a million dollars. Besides, where would Trigger have gotten it? Neil decided to start reading every page of the newspaper each day to see if any local robberies had been reported. Maybe inside the box was a huge old valuable vase or statue, Indian or Ancient Egyptian, dug up in some ruins by an archeologist and stolen from a museum. But why would Trigger take a thing like that? Maybe the police were looking for whatever it was right this minute. Maybe their clues would lead them straight to the Applewhites' toolshed. If that happened, who would get arrested? Neil, the Accessory, quivered under his covers. Trigger said he would come back every single day to check, that's how serious it was. Neil's thoughts spun around in circles until he fell asleep.

He woke up again before morning, as though jolted by an inner alarm. If Trigger — or the police — went prowling around the toolshed, then he, Neil, had to know about it. There was one way he could make sure. He fished around his bedside table until his fingers touched his flashlight. It was twenty-five minutes of three by his clock. Neil slid out of bed and put on his woolen bathrobe and loafers. Quietly he went into the bathroom and helped himself to a can of talcum powder. He sniffed it experimentally and a faint flowery scent filled his nostrils. Maybe that smell wouldn't be so noticeable outdoors. Real fingerprint powder didn't smell, he supposed, but this was the best he could do.

Neil crept down the carpeted stairs and out of the house into the dark cold morning. Something furry swished against his bare ankles and his heart nearly stopped beating. In the wavering beam of his flashlight, he caught sight of a golden streak and nearly laughed out loud.

"Saucie!" he whispered. Applesauce, their big yellow and white cat, had slithered out the kitchen door unnoticed and was now on a predawn prowl of the windy field where a few gnarled old pear trees bordered a low stone wall.

At the toolshed door, Neil flashed his light into the

window peephole he had rubbed clean, to get another look at the big box. Blankness hit his eyes. Trigger had covered the window from the inside with newspapers and there was no way to see in. Rats. Neil bent down and with scientist-like precision, sprinkled the talcum powder lightly across the full length of the wooden doorsill. For good measure, he also scattered some around the stiff, unruly blades of grass that grew against the step. It looked like frost.

Upstairs again, Neil propped his registration card for Judo lessons against his desk lamp. No danger of forgetting that! It was already filled out as far as he could go.

```
NAME Neil Applewhite  AGE 9¼
ADDRESS 65 Windsor Hill Rd.  TOWN Hawthorne
SCHOOL Kennedy  GRADE 4
```

I give my son permission to attend the
Beginners' Judo Class.

_____

Signature of Parent

Just one blank left. He'd ask Dad to sign first thing in the morning. (No point in asking Mom. To her, Judo was rough and risky.) Turning his pillow over, he gave it a couple of practice chops — Pow! — Pow! Then he went back to sleep.

2

A Tough Bargain

BREAKFAST! BREAKFAST, EVERYONE!" Jamie called. He banged on Neil's door and shouted, "Last one down is a chicken's uncle!"

Neil grabbed his bathrobe and pajamas from the floor, and jammed them onto a hanger in his closet. He shot his slippers in after them. The time had come to talk to Dad about Judo. Shouldn't take long, he figured, because how could any sensible father refuse to sign up for such a healthy, body-building, super-duper plan for his scrawny oldest son. With the YMCA envelope in hand, the unsigned registration card in his pants' pocket and a ballpoint pen clipped to his shirt pocket, he galloped downstairs, too late to catch up with the bounding Jamie.

"Morning, Mother," he beamed, plunging into the sunny kitchen and slamming into his ladder-back chair at the round pine table. "Dad down yet?"

"He'll be right in," Mother said. She was preparing

five breakfasts and three school lunches at the same time. The cafeteria at Kennedy was being enlarged, so, for the time being, the pupils had to bring their sandwiches from home and eat them in their classrooms, an arrangement they approved of because this way they could eat faster and get out to play sooner. "Dad's checking to see if the paper's here," Mother said. "Watch the toast, Neil, while Bonnie scrambles the eggs. Here's the wooden spoon, dear, just keep stirring them."

"I don't want my toast too brown," Bonnie said, glancing toward Neil at the counter. "How come you're so chipper?"

"This morning I'm going to get permission to become a Judo champ," Neil couldn't resist saying. "Then if you scotch my eggs, I'll be able to flip you through the air." Bonnie's blue eyes widened, and Mother looked up in alarm. "Flip *me!* Flip *me!*" Jamie said, setting his tumbler down so hard the orange juice splashed on his placemat.

"What's this?" Dad asked, as he came in with the morning paper and took his place at the table.

"Only teasing," Neil said hastily. The toast popped

up, and he had to start buttering it. "Listen, Dad, re-member those Judo lessons they're going to give at the Y? Remember how great they are and how strong you'd get? Well, I've decided to sign up, after all. There's still time and, boy, that's the kind of lessons I need. Here, read this over again, Dad." He laid out the mimeographed sheets on the breakfast table, leaving buttery fingerprints on them.

"I do recall," Dad said, putting on his reading glasses and studying the sheets carefully. Neil held his breath. He put more bread in the toaster and shoved down the lever with crossed fingers. No word from Dad. The silence was too long to stand. "Fish is taking Judo," Neil said to the cupboard door. "His father wants him to. To sharpen him up, you know. Make him tougher." Still silence. "We could practice together. Every day. You've got to practice to be any good." More silence. About to burst, Neil spun around and faced his father. "You just have to sign the registration card," he said. "I've filled out all the spaces but that. See? Right here." He dug the card out of his pocket and handed it to Dad along with the ballpoint pen.

"I see," Dad said. "You've convinced me, son. I

23

agree with you that Judo is an excellent sport. More-over, you'd get the proper supervision at the Y. How-ever," he added slowly, folding the sheets and putting them back in the envelope, "As you said, to be any good, you'd have to practice. To acquire a new ability, you'd have to stick with it." He took off his glasses and laid them on the newspaper.

Why did he take off his glasses before signing? Neil wondered. "Oh, I'd stick with it!" Neil said fervently. "I'd practice with Fish every single day. I promise. I'd stick with it like flypaper!"

Bonnie and Jamie laughed. Dad merely cocked his eyebrow and asked, "Now where have I heard that before?"

Neil flushed. He remembered very well making that exact same statement once before. It was last August, in fact, during their vacation at Cape Cod when they had spent a day in Plymouth. The *Mayflower II* was moored in the harbor, just like the first *Mayflower* that had anchored there in 1620, the bright sun shining on her square sails and painted sides. The Applewhites had explored her from forecastle to captain's cabin. Neil felt like a Pilgrim himself as he stood on the weathered main deck breathing the salty air and pretending to keep watch while the sea gulls wheeled over-head.

Later they headed for a local gift shop to get post-cards for their friends. In the souvenir-laden window, Neil spotted a ship model, minutely detailed, an exact replica of the ship they had just been on. He wanted it more than anything else he had seen all summer. The model wasn't for sale, a clerk told him, it could only be purchased unassembled in a large kit that included in-structions for putting together the many authentic-looking parts and pieces.

"Please let me get it," Neil implored his father. "I've spent this week's allowance and all my savings — ex-cept for $9.09 back home in my bank — for my snorkel and flippers. But if I don't get this *Mayflower* kit now, I can't get it, period. Please, Dad?"

"It's not the money," Dad answered. "I'll lend you that. What I'm interested in, is whether or not you'll have the patience to construct this model. Seems pretty complicated to me." He was examining the box as he spoke.

"Well, you know more about models that I do," Neil admitted. As an architect, Dad often made in-tricate models of the buildings he designed, and Neil had always liked looking at them in his office. "I'm sure I can do it. You said yourself I'm good with my hands. Mother, wouldn't that *Mayflower* model look groovy on the mantel at home?" He appealed to her because he could see she liked it, too.

"It really would, Neil," she smiled. "Let's give him a chance to prove he can do it," she said to Dad.

So the kit was bought with borrowed funds, and in the car, on the way back to their beach cottage, Neil studied the directions step by step. Bonnie, who had been strumming her guitar (she took it with her everywhere, even on day trips) said, "Listen, I just made up a song. It's called 'The Mayflower.'" She played a few notes and then began to sing:

> *"The winds are blowing,*
> *Storms and gales.*
> *The winds are blowing,*
> *Fill my sails.*
> *Goodby, old world,*
> *Goodby.*
>
> *"The sun is rising,*
> *Warm and bright.*
> *The sun is rising,*

Land in sight.
Hello, new world,
Hello."

"Hey, that's a good song," Jamie said. "Teach it to me so I can sing it, too."

"Not bad," Neil agreed. "You can both sing it to *my Mayflower* when I get her built. She's going to be a beauty."

"My only request is that you finish it," Dad said from the driver's seat. "When the going gets rough — 'Storms and gales' — and the newness wears off, you'll still have to stick with it."

"I'll stick with it like flypaper!" Neil had promised.

The remembered words echoed loud as a foghorn in Neil's mind. "The *Mayflower* model. I promised to stick with that," he said. "I paid you right back, Dad. And it's half done. More than half done, I'd say."

"What's left to do?" Dad asked.

"Let's see," Neil rubbed his chin. He took a gulp of milk and he spread more jam on his toast. It was weeks since he had worked on his model. "I cemented in the mizzen mast, so now I'm ready to start the rigging. That'll be the biggest job, I guess. I have to make the

27

sails and to paint the little Pilgrim figures and —
and things like that. You know, final touches here
and there."

"Suppose you finish that up first, before you tackle
something new."

"But Dad!" Neil protested, his voice rising in spite
of himself. "The deadline for registration is the fifteenth. And only ten boys can join that Judo class.
What if I'm not done in time and it's too late?"

"Neil, you're a great starter. As for 'sticking like
flypaper,' I've yet to see it. I'll make a bargain with
you — "

The telephone rang. Bonnie rushed across the
kitchen to answer it before the second ring. It was usually for her. Neil tried to swallow his eggs, impatiently
waiting for her to stop talking. It was old Janie again,
you might know. "My navy blue skirt," Bonnie was
saying. "Isn't that what we decided last night? The
green jumper? I don't know if the shirt that goes to
that is ironed yet. Wait a sec." She covered the
mouthpiece and asked, "Mom, is my candy-striped
shirt ironed yet? Jane says we ought to wear green today because we wore blue yesterday."

"It's in your closet," Mother said. "Now come back

here and finish your breakfast before it gets cold. Jamie, please stop feeding Saucie at the table. Get down, Saucie!" Applesauce was standing on her hind feet with her front paws on Jamie's knee, purring loudly as she bit into his crusts of cinnamon toast.

"Dad," Neil said. "The bargain? About Judo?" His hands felt cold and there was an anxious knot tightening in his stomach.

"Yes, Neil," Dad said, pushing back his chair. He took a last sip from his coffee cup and set it back in its saucer with a clink. "You finish the *Mayflower* model, son, and I will sign on the dotted line for your Judo lessons. Fair and square. The timing is up to you."

"Less than a week to get it done," Neil muttered, slumping on his elbow. "That's practically not possible. But I'll just *croak* if I can't take Judo."

"That," Dad said, rising from the table, "is the bargain. Take it or leave it."

"There's a place reserved on the mantel for the *Mayflower*," Mother said to encourage him. "And I'll be so glad when you're done, to get that awful card table out of your room. What a mess. I only wish I didn't think Judo was so dangerous."

Neil eyed her silently. No use going into that. To

him it was lots more dangerous *not* to take Judo. Only he couldn't tell her that. No use leaving out the registration card, either. Dad wasn't likely to change his mind. He put the envelope back in his pants pocket and said a dull "So long, Dad," to his father who was leaving for the office.

At quarter of eight Neil and Jamie left the house for school. "You start down the street, Jamie," Neil directed him, "And I'll catch up with you in a couple minutes. I've got to go back and see about something." He darted toward the barn before Jamie could protest.

Outwardly, the toolshed looked the same as usual. Crouching down, Neil examined the doorstep. In two places, the width of a shoe, the talcum powder was pressed and smudged. Trigger had already been here. "Whew!" Neil said, standing up. "That guy wasn't fooling." There wasn't time to fix up the step again and besides, Trigger would be in school all day. What the deuce was in that box?

Gathering up his books, Neil ran back to Jamie who was jumping up and down in a pile of autumn leaves right where Neil had left him. "Let's go, slowpoke, we should be halfway there by now." He took such long strides that Jamie had to trot to keep up with him.

Two or three times he growled, "Nuts!" and Jamie thought maybe he meant the acorns they were crunching underfoot. That was the only word Neil said for the winding mile it took them to reach the low brick building that was the Kennedy Grammar School. A bronze statue of Nathaniel Hawthorne stood on a granite base at the entrance to Hawthorne Park across the street. Jamie pointed out a squirrel sitting on top of Mr. Hawthorne's head like a fur hat, but Neil hardly noticed.

The first bell was clanging. Neil, careful to bypass Trigger in the crowded schoolyard, took his place in the fourth-grade line. Fish steamed up behind him, barely on time and puffing. "Didja get it signed?" he panted to Neil. "Didja Dad sign your Judo card?"

Neil shook his head.

"Aw heck," Fish said, his round face full of dejection. "How come?"

"Move along," Mr. Capaccio said briskly. "Let's go." He was short and stocky with red cheeks and long dark sideburns. Last year when he was in college, he was a pitcher on the state baseball team, which made him a pretty famous sports person. He was the one who coached the boys in football after school and, until yesterday, Neil wouldn't have missed practice for anything.

The class marched into the building and down the hall before Neil could whisper back, "Got to finish my ship model before he'll sign."

"Take long?" Fish asked.

"Not if I can help it," Neil said grimly.

As soon as the second bell rang, Mr. Capaccio said, "In your seats, everyone. With a sharpened pencil at the ready. Whittle your wits as well for a quiz we're going to have." Groans from the class. "It's on material we've already covered," Mr. Capaccio went on calmly. "Subject: the continent of Africa. Once known as the Dark Continent, but, hopefully, no longer so dark to you. You'll be surprised at how much you know."

Blank maps were handed out while he scrawled on the front chalkboard a long list of countries, cities, rivers, deserts and mountains to be located. With a rustling of papers and a shuffling of feet, they settled down.

Neil was making a cluster of dots for the Sahara region when a knock sounded at the door. All faces looked up. Mr. Capaccio, mildly curious, left his desk and opened the door. On the threshold stood Mrs. Applewhite in her brown suede jacket and green plaid slacks. Everybody in the whole room could see her.

Neil slouched down in his seat and bent his head so low his nose was almost touching his map. Maybe the big box in the toolshed had exploded, he thought, and Mother's here to get me before the police come. Maybe —

"Good morning, Mr. Capaccio," he heard his mother say, sounding natural enough. "I'm Mrs. Applewhite, Neil's mother."

"Yes, Mrs. Applewhite. I remember meeting you at the P.T.A. What may we do for you?"

"I'm sorry to disturb you," Mother said. "But I just discovered Neil forgot his lunch —"

Neil shut his eyes. His day had been so darkened by Dad's Judo bargain that he forgot his lunch. He remembered now the three brown paper bags lined up on the kitchen counter, each labeled by name and made to order — ham with cheese for Neil, ham with lettuce and mayonnaise for Bonnie, and peanut butter and jelly for Jamie. Well, he, Neil, would rather starve to death than have a relative show up at school and deliver his personal lunch to Mr. Capaccio in front of the whole class. No matter, he knew his mother devoutly believed if you didn't eat every last bite at mealtime, you'd be hospitalized with malnutrition by night. Parents! At least she had the good sense not to come in, and to leave without speaking to him. It was a relief to return to the sands of the Sahara, where he wished he could bury his head.

At three o'clock, when class was dismissed, Neil turned down Fish's neat idea to ride their bikes to Hawthorne Park and search for deserted birds' nests. Ordinarily he would have gone in a flash. "Nothing doing," he said. "I've got to get going on my ship model. You don't have to worry because you're all set for Judo, but not me. See you, Fish."

The first thing Neil had to do when he got home was to sprinkle a fresh supply of talcum powder on the toolshed step. Then, armed with a handful of chocolate chip cookies and a Coke, he shut himself in his room to tackle his long-neglected *Mayflower*. Before he could begin, though, he had to plough through all the junk on the card table.

"Clear the decks for action," he told himself. Getting started was the hardest part. A tottering stack of comic books had to be sorted out: one pile for Fish, one pile for Jamie. The rest, too worn out to read, were dumped in the wastebasket along with balls of dust and tattered old homework papers. He rescrewed the tops of his paint jars and lined them up in a row. Having to paint each tiny part of the model and then having to wait for it to dry before gluing it into place had slowed him down, that was the trouble. His paint brushes, caked with color, had to be cleaned in turpentine. List in hand, he checked his supply of working materials: scissors, tweezers, a spool of black thread, rigging thread, sand paper, a black crayon and masking tape. All there. These he arranged in an empty shoe box and its cover.

"Wow!" Neil said aloud, flopping in his desk chair and swishing around a sweater he was using as a dust-cloth. He had finally uncovered a nice bare working space on the card table. Ready, set, GO.

He got the directions out of his kit and looked for his place. Turning to page 11, which was headed "Final Assembly and Standing Rigging," he read:

> *Cement Fore Mast, Main Mast and Mizzen Mast assemblies into place on Main Deck.*

I've done that much, he thought, closely examining his

model to see that nothing had come unstuck. Now for —

"Telephone!" Bonnie said at his door. "For you, Neil, and it's not Fish and I don't know who it is, but he sure sounds mad."

Neil lurched to his feet. Trigger. Could be that Trigger had noticed the white talcum powder on the soles of his shoes. He waited for Bonnie to go back to her room before he said hello.

"You, there, Neil," Trigger said in a gruff voice. "I gotta talk to you and I want a straight answer."

"What about?"

"I saw your mother in the hall at school today. She report me to the principal? If you squealed on me —"

"Heck, no," Neil interrupted. "She just brought something I forgot. Nothing about you, fathead."

"You better be right, stinkweed. And get this, my orders still hold. Steer clear of that toolshed. Say — do you think it's gonna get much colder tonight?"

"I don't know," Neil said, caught by surprise. "How do I know? What do you want to know for?"

"None of your business," Trigger hung up.

Puzzled, Neil went back to the rigging directions. The paragraph he was studying instructed him to:

See page 9 for method of tying Blocks. Tie one Part 121 and one Part 122 to Bowsprit as shown. NOTE: *All standing Rigging Lines are crayon-blackened rigging thread. Draw all lines taut as possible without bending Masts. See Running Rigging Instructions (page 9) for method of seizing lines.*

A brainbuster, that's for sure, but he couldn't go on to the next step until he figured this one out. I'll get it, he thought, I'll get it because this is my end of the bargain. Judo Class, look out. And Trigger Deal, *you* look out. Here comes Neil Applewhite. One Judo Champion coming up!

3

Noises in the Night

NEIL WORKED on his *Mayflower* model until the evening newspaper arrived. He studied the weather report on the front page. It said:

> Mostly cloudy with occasional rain or drizzle chiefly nighttime and early morning hours through Thursday. Temperatures in the low 50s. Moderate easterly winds.

He read it again to make sure he wasn't overlooking a clue. No cold wave was predicted that he could see. Why should Trigger care if it got cold?

Neil scanned the first section for local robberies. None were reported. On a hunch he looked up Lost and Found to see if any of those items might possibly be in the big box. Two watches and one sapphire ring were listed. No soap there. Turning to the Sports page on his way to the comics, his eye lit on an action photo topped by the caption, "Judo Demonstration to be Aired on TV."

Leaning on his elbows, Neil pored over the picture of a Judo expert flinging a man upside down in midair. "Pictured above is Brown Belt Instructor Dick Grodin who will star on Sports Highlights Friday at 6:30 P.M. He will explain Judo principles and techniques. Local youths will participate in actual demonstrations. Don't miss this unusual feature."

Don't miss it! Neil wouldn't miss it for a trip to Mars. He hoped his whole family could see it together, especially Mom, because this would show her Judo at its best, better than he could ever explain it. He was itching to cut out the article for Fish right then and there, but he couldn't do that because it was still today's paper and no one else had read it yet. Reluctantly he folded it up and left it on the table in the family room.

Although it was only quarter past five, it was already dark outside. Heavy clouds mounded in the sky, and a shower of yellow leaves were pooled under the branchy rock maples. Neil went out to the toolshed with his flashlight in his hand and the can of talcum powder in his jacket pocket. Saucie was busy poking around the doorstep, her nose in the scattered powder and her tail aquiver. He stooped down to scratch her ear.

Rattle-Clunkety-Click!

Neil jumped. Saucie's fur stood on end and she hunched her back. "What's that?" Neil said out loud. He aimed his flashlight at the door handle of the tool-shed. There was no key in the lock and the knob was not moving. Gingerly he touched the cold brass knob and turned it. Locked, tighter than a drum. Yet sure as shooting, he had heard the sound of that door being unlocked. Not loud, but clear as day.

Rattle-Clunkety-Click!

There it was again! Frowning, he tried harder to open the door, yanking hard as he turned the knob. Locked. Beats me, he thought, maybe I'm hearing things. He scooped up Saucie and rubbed his chin in her thick yellow fur. But you heard it too, I know you did. Kinda scary!

"Neil! Hey, Neil!" That was Fish's voice. It wasn't coming out of the toolshed. It was coming from the back porch.

"Hi, Fish. Be right with you." Neil waved his light and ran up toward the house. Saucie skittered away behind the lilac bushes.

"Got something to show you," Fish said as Neil came up the steps. He was flapping a paper as he spoke.

"I tried to call you but your line was busy." (That Bonnie!) "It's about Judo. A whole program about Judo on TV. Friday night. Flash your light on this. Look."

"Yeah, terrific!" Neil said. "I saw it. They're going to show actual demonstrations. Maybe we'll get some good ideas so we can start practicing before the class gets going. The sooner the better, I always say."

"Me, too. What could we use for a gym, though? We'd need lots of space. And some gym mats."

"My garage," Neil said, meaning the old barn. "There's plenty of room in there." On a second thought, he changed his mind; he didn't want Trigger to catch him practicing Judo. "Or how about yours?" he asked.

"Nifty. My folks won't mind. They're all hung up on how healthy exercise is. For me, not them."

"Then all we have to get hold of is some gym mats. I'll look around the house to see if there's anything we could use."

"Me too. Gotta go now. See you, Neil."

"So long, Fish. And thanks."

For the rest of the evening, Neil was quiet and preoccupied. He couldn't stop thinking about the sounds he had heard at the toolshed. He was positive Trigger hadn't been inside because he would have surely come out and clobbered him for snooping around. When his homework was finished, he sat at the card table in his room and tied the rigging line from the bowsprit to the foremast of the *Mayflower*. It was like trying to make a spider's web, only worse. Using both single and special blocks according to the instructions, it took him many tries and a lot of sputtering to get the tiny knots correctly in place. He was beginning to wish the Pilgrims had never left home.

One last time, before going to bed, he decided to go back out to the toolshed. His ears had been playing tricks on him. How could he have heard the lock unlocking? Impossible. Only Trigger had the key. Trigger had scared him into doubting his own senses, that's what. Well, he'd see about that. It was starting to rain. Big cold drops pelted the shingled roofs and spattered the dry leaves that matted the ground. Neil tapped against the windowpane of the toolshed door. Listening hard, he heard nothing but the rain and a rising gust of wind. He rattled the doorknob and there was no unlocking sound. The rain would soon wash away his talcum powder, too bad about that, but at least his ears were clear and he wasn't loony after all.

Heaving a sigh, he turned to leave. A rough voice crackled after him, *"Listen, don't give up the ship!"* It came from inside the toolshed, the voice of a cross old man.

Neil clapped his hand over his mouth. He stopped breathing, shoulders hunched and feet rooted to the ground. He stared at the motionless door and waited numbly. Struck by lightning, that's what he thought.

Time passed, the rain fell, no one spoke.

"Wh — What did you say?" Neil whispered. He took two steps closer to the door (was the door locked?) A little louder, "Did you call me?"

Applesauce, appearing from nowhere, backed against him, her ears flattened, her tail twitching. Neil inched within touching distance of the doorknob. "Is anyone in there?" It was unbelievable that Trigger would lock a *person* in there with his big box. Maybe it was old Mr. Pike from Potter's Market!

Neil sprang forward, turning the knob and banging on the window. "Mr. Pike, are you in there? It's me, Neil Applewhite. Are you locked in there?"

"Listen, don't give up the ship!" The same cranky voice, the same warning.

"Is that you, Mr. Pike?" Neil shouted.

Rattle-Clunkety-Click!

The mechanical sound suddenly made Neil wonder if a record player was making these noises. Maybe some crazy mechanism got set off by the lowered temperature. Maybe —

Rattle-Clunkety-Click!

Applesauce meowed and scratched frantically at the doorsill. By now Neil was certain a person wasn't inside. Whatever cockeyed thing it was, he couldn't figure it out now. He checked to make sure the door was locked, listening a while longer. The wind swept some twigs against his legs and the rain was blowing in his face, rolling down inside his collar. Shivering, Neil gathered up Applesauce and headed for the house. He hung up his soaking jacket and kicked off his muddy shoes.

"Where have you been?" Bonnie asked on her way to the kitchen.

"Forgot to put away my bike," he mumbled. He half expected her to tell him his sopping hair had turned snow white (such things were possible, he had read, out of sheer fright).

Until he fell asleep, the locking noises and that

scratchy message about the *Mayflower* whirled in his ears, over and over again, a jumble of sounds making no sense.

Thursday morning dawned gray and drizzly as predicted. Neil, buckled into his yellow sou'wester, avoided going near the toolshed. A furtive glance in that direction assured him that it was still standing, ordinary as ever. Which doesn't fool me, he thought, that spooky mysterious thing inside is Trigger's problem and he can have it. "Come on, Jamie, I'll race you to the corner!" Neil said. It felt so good to run in the chilled wet air that he almost forgot to let Jamie win.

It was still pouring at noontime, no chance for an outdoor recess. When the 11:30 bell rang, Mr. Capaccio said, "Neil Applewhite and Barton Fisher." Both boys scrambled to their feet. "Your turn today to get the milk cartons and the ice cream cups. Just make sure you get the boxes marked Room Six. O.K. for the rest of you to get out your lunches."

Neil and Fish marched out of the room with responsible-looking faces. Once outside, they whacked each other gleefully on the shoulders and shoved each other down the hall. That Cappy was sure one great teacher. "Any ideas for gym mats?" Fish asked.

Neil shook his head. He had forgotten to look around.

"Me, neither. We've got plenty of pillows at our house, but no spare ones I can have."

In the cafeteria a long line of pupils from the other grades stood waiting for their cartons. At the counter there was a mixup about an unmarked box and the contents had to be recounted. As they straggled into place, Neil and Fish inspected the new wing that was being added to enlarge the cafeteria.

"Sawdust!" Neil said. "Piles and piles of sawdust."

"What about it?" Fish asked.

"We could use it for gym mats. Stuff old pillowcases with sawdust. Or laundry bags. You know, make our own."

"Terrif! There's heaps of it — just lying around. Where are the workmen?"

"Out to lunch, I guess," Neil said, craning his neck. "Anyway, I don't see any. Do you?"

"Nope. But they wouldn't mind if we took some. It'd help them clean the place up."

"We'd be doing them a favor," Neil agreed. "Look, maybe we could get enough now to make a practice mat — put it in a pillowcase or something and if that works, get lots more sawdust at the lumberyard."

"Cool."

"You keep my place in line and I'll slide over there and fill up my pockets. If anyone comes along, whistle. Then I'll stand in line while you go."

Neil slipped through the dismantled doorway and hastily scooped up as much of the yellow sawdust from the floor as he could. When his pockets were bulging, he swept handfuls of sawdust from a worktable into his sweater, glad for once that he was skinny because there was plenty of room inside. Feeling like a walking beanbag, he sidled back to the milk line which was slowly moving up, and changed places with Fish. Fish filled his pockets with sawdust and also his stretch socks. There was no extra room in his shirt.

"Tickles," he said to Neil on their way back to Room Six.

"Yeah," Neil said, wiggling his stomach. "And this darned box keeps slipping. I've got to pick it up over again to get a better grip. You go ahead."

Once he had the box clasped in his arms more securely, Neil looked up to see Trigger coming down the hall with one of his seventh-grade buddies. They blocked his way and stared at him.

"Well, if it isn't lumpy-dumpy stinkweed," Trigger said. "You got baseballs in your pockets or what?" He gave Neil's pants pocket a whack with his knuckles and a cloud of sawdust puffed out. "Hey, this little dolly's got sawdust insides!" The two of them hooted and joined in the game of poking Neil, who was clutching the box of milk cartons. He shot his foot out to kick at them and at the same moment, got pushed in the chest. His feet skidded out from under him and he toppled to the floor. The milk cartons plopped around him like snowballs.

"You dropped something," Trigger said. They stepped over Neil as though he were a puddle and went snickering down the hall.

The third-grade door burst open and Miss Mudgett came popping out, her head floating over Neil like a pink balloon. "What's going on?" she demanded. She was short and plump and very excitable. "What are you doing down there, Neil Applewhite? And where did all this sawdust come from? Are they packing milk cartons in sawdust these days? Goodness gracious!"

Neil groped his way up to a standing position and leaned against the wall. "I tripped," he said. "Sorry, Miss Mudgett. I'll clean this stuff up —"

"You'll stay right there — you're shedding!" In a flurry of directions, she assigned a fleet of third-graders, giggling and eager, to the rescue. Two boys were picking up the milk cartons and putting them in the box. A girl was sent to the supply closet for a broom and dustpan, another was put in charge of the chattering classroom. Miss Mudgett herself got a whisk broom from her desk drawer and vigorously at-tacked the sawdust covering Neil's clothes.

"It's hardly any use," she heaved after several minutes of work. "You've still got as much as ever and now it's all over me, too." She looked down at her navy wool dress and shook the hem of her skirt. Neil didn't mention the sawdust that sprinkled her teased white hair like corn flakes.

"Well, thanks, anyway," Neil said. "At least I can sweep up the floor. Could — could somebody please take the milk down to Grade Four? Lunch must be al-most over."

"Yes, yes, of course," Miss Mudgett flushed. "I should have thought of that before. I know! I'm going to get some sticky tape. That'll fix my dress. I suggest you do the same, Neil, when you get home." She scurried off in a mist of sawdust, murmuring to herself

"Goodness gracious!" and "Oh, dearie me!"

Mr. Capaccio eyed Neil with interest when he finally returned. "Heard about your mishap," he commented. "Funny you should get a box packed with sawdust. Know how that happened?"

Neil shook his head. He opened his mouth and closed it again.

"Perhaps you'd rather tell me about it after class. Eat your lunch now, before the milk gets any warmer."

After class, Neil, alone with Mr. Capaccio at his desk, told him the honest truth about the sawdust. How he was going to use it for a gym mat and how much he wanted to take Judo. He left Trigger's name out because he couldn't go into that, no matter what. Mr. Capaccio thought Judo was a spendid sport, although he'd never learned it himself. He, too, had seen the picture on the Sports page and was going to watch the program Friday night. He recommended, however, that Neil give up the sawdust idea as less than practical. They shook hands and that neat guy Cappy said "Good luck." Any other teacher would have given him detention.

Thinking it over, on the way home, Neil wished

he'd been able to tell Mr. Capaccio about the noises in the toolshed, to find out what his theories would be and how he would explain it. Even at this safe distance it was hard to think straight. It couldn't be magic, it must be real. Some kind of recorder or computer or even mind-reading robot (how else could it have known about his ship?) must be in Trigger's big box. The cold night air had somehow set off the sensitive machinery. This strange instrument was so intricate that Trigger had to check it every day. That much was certain. And it was worth "a lot of dough." Trigger had said so. *A secret invention!* That's what it was. Trigger had stolen an inventor's secret invention and was hiding it in the Applewhites' toolshed till the inventor could buy it back.

The rain had stopped and the clearing sky was a bright golden gray. The tree trunks glistened wetly and the withered grass sparkled with beads of water. Neil breathed in the newly washed air and felt light-headed with relief. A flock of wild geese honked over his head and he pumped his arm at them, waving good-by. "Have a good trip," he yelled.

Now all he had to do was find the inventor (in the

Yellow Pages, probably; there couldn't be many) and tell him not to worry. He started to run. Home was in sight.

Neil stopped short in his tracks. A police car was parked out front of the Applewhites' house.

4

Free Gym Mats

NEIL WASN'T the least bit surprised. Still, he stared with much interest at the familiar police car as he walked slowly by. It was Car 2, Town of Hawthorne, a '71 Chevy. The blue light on the roof wasn't flashing and if the radio was working, he couldn't hear it. He wondered if he'd have to sit alone in the back seat or if they'd let him sit up front. He'd never ridden in a police car before.

He went, as he usually did, up the gravel driveway and in by the back door. Dumping his schoolbag in the hall, he decided he might as well leave his jacket on — why take it off if he was going to the police station. Besides, he didn't want to have to explain the sawdust all over his sweater (maybe nobody'd notice his speckled pants.) Subdued voices were coming from the living room: the policeman must be in there. He had no idea what was going to happen next.

"That you, Neil?" Mother called. "Come on in, dear. You're late today."

"Had to see Mr. Capaccio after class," he answered. He hung back by the doorway, avoiding the eyes of Mother and Jamie. They were standing in the middle of the room with a husky young policeman, a tall dark figure in his close-fitting uniform. He had a ruddy complexion and a thatch of stiff blond hair, cut short. The three turned toward Neil.

"Hello, Officer Kroznick," Neil managed to say. "You been waiting for me?"

"Well, no — but I'm glad to see you anyhow." He took a stride in Neil's direction and gave him a bone-cracking handshake. "How ya been?"

Jamie was prancing up and down, bursting with news. "Bonnie had an accident, and she went to the hospital in a *police* car — with the *siren* on!"

Neil sagged down on the arm of the nearest chair. He blinked at Jamie in bewilderment.

"Hush, hush," Mother said, patting Jamie's cheek. "Don't alarm Neil like that. Bonnie's home now and she's fine, just fine. Thanks to our good friend here."

"Always glad to help," Officer Kroznick grinned. His boomy voice filled the room.

"We mustn't keep you any longer," Mother said. "It was so kind of you to stop by to see how Bonnie's doing. I know her father will be as grateful as I am for your interest."

Mother and Jamie went with him to say good-by while he put on his cap and leather gloves. When the front door closed, Jamie ran to the living room window to watch him drive away in the police car.

Neil had collapsed haphazardly into the wing chair, his head flung back and his legs dangling over the arm. "What happened?" he asked weakly. "Bonnie O.K.?"

Mother, absently brushing at Neil's sawdusty knees, said, "Thank heavens, yes. But what a day this has been. Around ten this morning, the school nurse called me to say Bonnie'd hurt her ankle and that she ought to have x rays right away. She wanted my permission to have Officer Kroznick drive her over to the hospital in the police car. When I got to the Emergency Room, Bonnie was already there and Doctor Edwards was taking care of her. No bones broken —"

"*That's* a lucky break!" Jamie said, doubling up with laughter at his own joke. "Get it, Neil? Mommy said —"

"Yeah, I get it. That's funny. Go on, Mom."

Mother smiled at Jamie, shaking her head wearily. "Poor Bonnie. It's a severe sprain and very painful. No matter how hard she tried, she simply couldn't stand on it. So Doctor Edwards put a cast on. She'll have to use crutches for a couple days, at least till the metal heel on the bottom of the cast hardens in. Then she'll be able to manage pretty well. We see the doctor in two weeks for a check-up — I must jot that down."

"And she won't have to go to school till Monday," Jamie added. He pounced onto Neil to tickle him and Neil rolled him off onto the floor with a ferocious growl. He was beginning to feel very good.

"No fooling in the living room," Mother said automatically, as she grabbed the brass lamp which nearly toppled over when Jamie's toe hit the slender leg of the antique table. She adjusted the parchment shade with a critical glance, saying, "Neil, why don't you say hello to Bonnie if she's not sleeping. She's in the family room on the couch. And take off your jacket — you'll roast in there. We lit the fireplace because it seemed cozier for her. I'll be in the sunroom weaving napkins if she wants me."

"Tell him Fish called up," Jamie reminded her.

"Oh yes, twice. He sounds very excited about some-thing he wants to tell you. Come on, Jamie, I'll let you sort some spools for me."

"You awake?" Neil asked, poking his head in the family room. He had hung up his jacket and taken off his sweater which he'd stuffed in his schoolbag. His shirt didn't look half-bad.

"Hi." Bonnie was propped up on the couch with a mound of pillows at her back and a patchwork quilt over her legs. A pair of varnished crutches were lean-ing against the nearest chair. She was idly flicking the pages of a magazine on her lap in the light of the leap-ing flames behind the firescreen. Neil could smell the scent of burning applewood and pine cones.

"What have you been up to?" he asked, coming in. He plunked himself down on the braided rug by the couch. "What'd you do to get that ride in a police car? With a siren blasting away."

"Look it!" Bonnie said. With an impish wag of her hand, she flung back the quilt and displayed a fat white cast that enclosed her left leg from her toes to her knee.

"My gosh!"

"It's only a sprain," she said airily, swinging back

her long hair. "Nothing much, really. But at first I thought I'd broken it to pieces. Wowie, did it ever hurt! Do you want to hear all the gory details?"

"That's what I'm trying to find out."

"Well, we had Science this morning and Mr. Lyon took our class and the third-period class over to Hawthorne Park —"

"In the rain?"

"Oh, sure, we voted to go, rain and all. There's lots of different trees over there and we're supposed to learn how to identify them without their leaves."

"Sounds like more fun than being cooped up in a stuffy old classroom."

"That part's fun, all right. Anyway, we were all standing around a little pond — you know, the one behind the rose gardens — and we were looking at a ginkgo tree (that's Chinese) when this boy from the third-period class — he was standing next to me but I didn't notice him — all of a sudden, he said, 'See what I've got.' He had something in his hands and when he opened them up, a *frog* jumped out! Right at *me!*"

Neil kept a straight face by staring hard at Bonnie's toes sticking out of the big white cast.

"The frog hit me and jumped off. I didn't even know what it was at first. Except it was alive and might bite."

"Then what?"

"Then I screamed, acourse. I backed up as fast as I could and my foot slipped into a little hollow I never saw and I fell down. My ankle got twisted under me and I couldn't stand up and everybody was jamming around. It was awful. I didn't cry exactly, only my nose was running and my hands and clothes were all mucky — ugh! So then Mr. Lyon and some of the others carried me out to his car and he drove me back to school. He let Janie ride with me. The school nurse examined my ankle in her office and by then it was so swollen you couldn't even see my ankle bones. It'd turned all purpley-pink like the color of bubble gum — chewed."

"So that's what you had to do to get a ride in a police car."

"Big deal. Officer Kroznick was real nice, though. And you know what? He drove right through a red light on Main Street."

"Cool. Hey, what happened to the guy? The one with the frog who started this?"

"I didn't tell on him," Bonnie said hastily. "Some-body else saw it happen and they reported him to Mr. Lyon when he started asking questions. He was really kind of cute. That boy, I mean. Not counting the frog part."

"Well, take it easy," Neil said, standing up and stretching. "I gotta go call Fish. Want anything to eat?"

"No thanks," Bonnie said. "You can put another log on the fire, though."

Fish called again before Neil had a chance to call him. "How'd you make out at school?" Fish asked. "Did Cappy rank you out about the sawdust?"

"Nope, he was O.K. But that sawdust idea won't work —"

"Who cares?" Fish said grandly. "Lissen, this is what I gotta tell you. Gram says we can have the cush-ions from her old porch glider. For our Judo mats."

"Super!"

"We can go get 'em anytime we want. You wanna go now?"

"You bet. I'll do my *Mayflower* later. Be right over, Fish."

Neil hung up, feeling better and better. Maybe my

luck's changing, he thought. He got out the telephone book and looked up *Inventors* in the Yellow Pages. No such animal. However, between *Insurance-Savings Banks* and *Interior Decorators*, he noticed a small section called *Intercommunication-Equipment, Systems and Service.* That's it! Several companies with names that sounded like kids' games, were listed, but Neil didn't have time to study them. He'd have to get back to this tonight. At least he knew he was on the right track — finally. His luck *was* changing.

Before leaving the yard, Neil knocked on the tool-shed door, his ear pressed against the windowpane. Not a sound inside. Hope that thing in the box still works, he thought. He knocked again with no result. Oh well, first things first. He was on his way to get the Judo mats.

Although Fish's house was within sight of the Applewhites' house, Neil rode his bike, in case he might need it. Fish was standing outside the open double garage, red-faced and puffing. "Been clearing out a space for us," Fish said. "Lookit. Think that's enough room?" Barrels, cartons, garden implements and baskets of all sizes were shoved in unsteady piles against the walls and in the center, a bare patch of concrete was ready and waiting for the mats.

"Couldn't be better," Neil said, surveying their half of the garage with a toothy grin.

"Leave your bike here. We can't ride bikes and carry cushions. Besides, it's not far to walk if we take the short cut."

"Suits me. Let's go."

They dogtrotted down the street, crossed over at the second corner and went through the dentist's backyard to the edge of some straggly woods. They followed a rocky footpath, so crooked and overgrown that in some places they had to walk single file. The path opened onto a wide field. Cutting diagonally to the sidewalk, they landed on Oak Street, three places away from Gram Fisher's brown shingled house with white trim and a spacious front porch.

"She got company?" Neil asked. An ancient Model T Ford was parked in front. It was black and shiny and its spoked wheels glistened under curving mud guards.

"Don't know. Something must be going on. Let's go in the side door — that's always open."

Neil followed Fish, after they scuffled their muddy boots on the doormat, into a small entry between the kitchen and dining room.

"Hi, Gram!" Fish shouted. "She's kinda harda hearing. Gram! Hi, there, Gram!"

"Hello, boys! Hello!" Gram bustled in and squeezed them both in her plump arms. Her fluffy white hair looked sort of like Albert Einstein's, Neil thought, and she wore real granny glasses. "I didn't mean to keep you waiting," she said, "but, oh mercy me, my dear friend has lost her pet and I'm doing my best to console her."

"I know how bad that feels," Neil said with a pang for Gypsy.

"I'm sorry, too." Fish said. "Want us to come back later?"

"Gracious, no child. If you don't mind getting them out yourselves. Did your mother tell you I bought a new glider at Sears, in that after-summer sale they had? Truly a bargain. So I've got no use for the old one. It's down cellar on the left-hand side next to the water heater. Covered with a sheet. Take what cushions you want, you're more than welcome."

"Gee, thanks a whole lot," Neil said.

"If you want to know, I'm pleased as punch to be asked. Now tell me again, dear, what's the name of that new game you want them for — Jumbo, is it?"

"JUDO, Gram," Fish said loudly. "JUDO. It's ancient Japanese and when we learn it, we'll give you a demonstration, huh, Neil."

"We sure will."

"Fancy that. You're fairly hopping to get started, I can see. So go along with you. I must be getting back to my poor friend. Bye-bye for now."

Neil and Fish went down the steep wooden steps and peered around the dimly lit cellar. It was like a stone cave filled with odd and shadowy shapes.

"I see it!" Fish said, shoving aside a wicker porch rocker and stumbling over some screens. "There it is."

"She said it was covered with a sheet," Neil said doubtfully. "That's a yellow bedspread."

"What's the diff? Hey, look at those cushions!" They were firm and taut, broadly striped and bouncy.

"They don't look so old to me."

"That's because she takes such good care of everything," Fish explained. "She and Gramps don't wear stuff out like us. You know that dining room table she's got upstairs? It's a hundred years old and they haven't worn it out yet."

"Well, you oughta know. They're nifty all right."

"You said it. Let's get this one out first."

Once they got the cushions upstairs and out of the house, it took them a while to arrange a practical way of transporting their bulky cargo. Each wound up carrying a back cushion under his left arm and one end of the long seat cushion under his right. The third back cushion had to be balanced on top of the seat cushion and it was a big bother because it kept falling off.

They marched in step over to the open field and into the wet woods where the narrow bumpy path threw them offstride. Jouncing along, they clung to the cushions, tightening their grasp to keep them from slipping. It was a slow trip to Fish's garage.

"Finally! Our private gym," Neil beamed, dropping his end of the seat cushion onto the floor and the other one onto that. It felt great to swing around freely and unwind.

"With practically professional mats," Fish said, flopping full length onto the pile of cushions.

"Let's put 'em in place. We can start training today."

"No, no, no!" Fish's mother came running into the garage, clutching a sweater over her shoulders with one hand and flapping her other arm as though she were stopping traffic.

"What's wrong, Mom?" Fish asked, abruptly sitting up.

"What's wrong!" She hauled Fish off the cushion and pointed to it. "Pick that up. Get it off the floor. Immediately. If you please."

Neil and Fish rushed to do as they were told, stooping to grab hold of the other cushions as well. "You said we could use the garage —" Fish began.

"Honey, I said you could use the garage and you can. But not with Gram's brand-new cushions. Why, they haven't even been *sat* on yet! I saw them going by from the kitchen window and I couldn't believe it. There must be some mistake."

"Our fault," Neil said. "We got them out of the cellar ourselves. Guess we didn't look around hard enough. It was kinda dark down there."

"We'll take 'em right back," Fish said. "If we can still have the others for our gym. Think we can?"

"These look O.K. to you?" Neil asked.

Mrs. Fisher inspected the cushions on all sides for dirt and oil spots. "No harm done," she said at last. "Put them in the hallway and Dad can take them back tonight in the car. It'll save you that long walk again."

"I'd justa soon go now. If we can still have the old ones. How about you, Neil?"

"Oh, let's go now. We gotta get our gym in shape." Neither of them happened to explain about their short-cut because Mrs. Fisher might think that way was too sloppy for the brand-new cushions. "Don't drop them," she warned as she went back to the house. "I'll give Gram a call to tell her you're coming. And how come."

Neil and Fish started out again, getting in step like trained moving men. At the sound of someone shrieking loud as a siren, they turned their heads to see Jamie running toward them at top speed.

"Whattaya doing?" Jamie asked, coming to a stop by colliding into the seat cushion. "I'm a policeman and I wanta know whattaya doing?"

"Watch it," Neil said sharply. "You'll knock this out of our hands if you're not careful. We're taking these over to Fish's Gram's house."

"Can I come?"

"Not now, Jamie. We're busy —"

"Say, maybe he could carry one of these cushions," Fish said. "Here, Jamie, take this and see if you can walk with it."

Jamie's face brightened. He hugged the cushion to his chest, his eyes barely peeping over the top of it. "Sure I can. See?" He strutted up and down to show them. "Now can I come?"

Fish and Neil exchanged glances. No need to tell Jamie about their gym, but he would be a big help if he could manage to lug one of those cushions. "He can rest before we start back with the other ones." Neil said.

"They'll probably be saggier than these ones and easier to carry," Fish said.

"Well, O.K., if you want to," Neil told the hopefully waiting Jamie. "Go tell Mom you're coming with me. We'll wait for you." Jamie scooted off.

"He can take that extra cushion," Fish planned. "And we'll take the others."

"Right. Glad to have him aboard. The more cushion-carriers the better."

"I was a dope to pick out the wrong glider. You said —"

"Forget it. We can't squawk. We're still getting free gym mats for our gym."

"Here he comes now."

"Mom says yes," Jamie panted. "And oh, Neil, guess who was in our yard. Trigger Deal! I saw him myself. Over by the toolshed. And I said 'You want my brother?' and he said 'Get lost, kid,' " — this in a growly, Papa Bear voice — "And you know what? I did!"

"What d'ya s'pose *he* wanted?" Fish asked curiously.

"Search me," Neil shrugged, feeling a lead sinker hit his insides. "Come on, let's go."

Fish led the parade carrying his end of the glider seat cushion plus one cushion under his other arm and Neil followed, doing the same. Jamie brought up the rear, looking like a green-striped cushion walking by itself.

"Let's make-pretend we're an ambulance," Jamie called out. "And I'm the siren."

"And I'm the flashing red light," Neil said.

"And I'm the driver," Fish said. "I'm stepping on the gas right now."

"And here we go!" Jamie said, his short legs scurrying to keep up.

This is the way to travel, Neil thought, I'll take this old ambulance instead of a police car any day.

5

Sarsaparilla

My arms feel all tired out like spaghetti," Jamie complained.

"We're almost there," Fish said. "Hang on through this gloppy field and you'll be there. Honest."

"Wait till you see the funny old-fashioned car out front of Gram's," Neil said. "It's shiny as new. You'll like that."

"I see Gram's house and I don't see any funny old car," Jamie said, stopping for good and dropping his cushion on the sidewalk. "What'd you make me come for? I'm going home."

"Jamie, come back! I'll take your cushion, but you stay with us. Look, there's Gram now, on the porch. See, she's waving at you."

They struggled up the steps to the front door. Gram, talking a mile a minute, invited them in and helped them stack their cushions in the front hall.

"Shame on me for not seeing to it that you got the

right cushions for your Jumbo," she exclaimed. "I went right down and got the others for you and put them in the side entry. Now you take a seat in the parlor, do, and rest your weary bones. There's cupcakes aplenty *here* — poor Hattie Atkins couldn't eat a thing. Do you prefer fudge frosting or vanilla with sprinkles?"

She sat opposite them in her upholstered rocker, arms folded and ankles crossed, watching them eat with a pleasure that matched their own. Her white hair fanned back and forth as she rocked.

"Where did the funny old-fashioned car go?" Jamie asked between mouthfuls. He was glad he stayed.

"You must mean Hattie Atkins'. Poor dear thing, she went on home, dreading that empty house without her pet. She lives all sole alone, you know, twenty-one rooms and no Sarsaparilla for company."

"Sarsaparilla!" Jamie repeated. "That's a good name for a dog!"

Gram stopped rocking. "Oh, not a dog, dear," she said. "A parrot. Sarsaparilla's her parrot and she's been missing since way last Tuesday."

A missing *parrot!* So that's what the "secret invention" was!

A surge of laughter engulfed Neil like a tidal wave. He couldn't help himself. The harder he tried to stop, the more it bubbled up inside him.

"It isn't funny, young man," Gram said sadly. "Mrs. Atkins was most attached to that parrot. Why, it was practically a *person* to her. She could hardly feel worse if she'd lost a relative."

Neil nodded violently, his mouth clamped against the chuckles in his throat. Fish nudged him with his elbow and said loudly to Gram, "He's laughing at a joke I told him. He just caught on."

Again Neil nodded. He rubbed his eyes and sniffled somewhat, straightened up his face and said, "Sorry, Mrs. Fisher. Gosh, I wasn't laughing on account of Mrs. Atkins losing her pet. It wasn't that."

"Worse than lost," Gram said. "Stolen! Stolen in her cage right out of the kitchen. Now what scoundrel would dare do such a cruel thing, I'd like to know. It's a very mysterious case."

"Tell us what happened," Fish said.

"I guess it's all right to," Gram said hesitantly. "You see, Tuesday afternoon Hattie Atkins had an open house for Nellie Nugent who's running for the School Committee. I went myself. There must have been thirty to thirty-five people there, not all at once, but coming and going, as people do. Between us, we put on our thinking caps and tried to remember every single person present. Hat has the list and she's gotten in touch with most of them by now, trying to get an inkling as to what went on — right under her nose, so to speak. Some remember seeing Sassy and some don't. Well, to tell you the truth, not everybody takes to that bird — she's snappy, sometimes — but the majority, myself included, found her most entertaining. Most entertaining, indeed." She paused to smile at her recollections of Sarsaparilla.

"Did she talk?" Fish wanted to know.

"Polly want a cracker?" Jamie said.

"Better than that," Gran sniffed. "She could say a number of catchy things, mainly nautical. And she imitated sounds fit to kill!"

Neil clutched his sides in an effort to keep down another surge of uncontrollable laughter. (*Rattle-Clunkety-Click!*) Fish gave him a queer look.

"Years ago," Gram said, "Sassy belonged to Hattie Atkins' brother, Ben, who trained that parrot almost from babyhood. He was an invalid, poor soul, with time on his hands and patience by the yard. When he passed on, Hattie kept her. Talk about your feathered friend! That's Sarsaparilla to a T."

"And nobody knows what happened to her?" Fish asked.

"Well, this is the most terrible part." Gram's words dropped almost to a whisper. "Yesterday at a quarter of five, when Hattie Atkins was putting some potatoes on to boil, the phone rang and this voice — it was young, she said, and nervous-like — this voice said, 'I've got your parrot. If you want it back, you listen to me. Put fifteen dollars — all ones — in an envelope. Put that envelope in the flower pot on your porch. That's a lot of bills and I'm going to count them to make sure they're all there, so no tricks. No snooping around, neither. Not if you want your parrot back!' And then before she could even collect her wits to answer — she was quaking that hard — he hung up. Slam! In her ear."

Neil hunched forward. "Did she do it? Did she put the fifteen dollars out?"

"Well, yes and no," Gram answered. "Naturally

she didn't have any fifteen one-dollar bills in her purse or in the cookie jar. Only John D. Rockefeller would have that many one-dollar bills lying around the house. She got together five ones and then next morning she went over to Wally's Garage and had him change a ten-dollar bill for her. So she got the money all right, fifteen one-dollar bills like that wretched person told her to. She put them in a plain brown envelope and sealed it up."

"And then?"

"Then she didn't know where to put it!"

"In the flower pot on the porch!" the three boys said at once.

Gram shook her head. "Easier said than done. Do you know where Hattie Atkins lives? In that huge ark of a house that faces Berkshire Road. You must know it — the old Atkins homestead?"

Neil knew the one. His father always called it the Gingerbread House because of its fancy scroll-saw decorations. A showplace of the past, with its towers and balconies, balustrades and turrets, it now stood in weathered disrepair in a grove of tall dark pines.

"There's the back porch," Gram explained, counting on her fingers, "the side porch, the front veranda, the balcony off the dining room, and, if you care to call it a porch, that place outside the conservatory. Now, tell me, where would *you* put the fifteen dollars?"

They knit their brows in concentration. "Where the flower pots are!" Neil said.

"They're all over the place," Gram said hopelessly. "Hat has a green thumb and there's no stopping her when it comes to planting and transplanting and what not. My gracious, how those plants flourish and bloom, you never saw the likes of it. But she doesn't bother much about the empty pots and they do pile up."

"Where's the money now, then?" Fish asked.

"That's the trouble. She keeps moving it from porch to porch. Granted, that bird-napper must have had one particular place in mind, but who knows which? Every time she looks (and she's trying hard not to snoop) the envelope is right where she left it."

"Maybe when she got home from your house this afternoon," Neil said, full of wishful thinking, "maybe the money was gone and Sarsaparilla was back."

"Just what we had hoped! But no siree. She phoned before you got here to say the money was still in the pot where she'd put it. So she switched it again to another porch. This dreadful waiting is such a strain on the nerves."

"I know what!" Jamie said. "Tell her to call up Officer Kroznick. He'll drive over to her house in his police car and he'll catch that bird robber."

"If only she would," Gram sighed. "She won't, though. Hattie Atkins is stubborn as a mule when her mind's made up. She's going to handle this in her own sweet way, and there's no budging her. All she cares about is Sarsaparilla, safe and sound. Nothing else. Myself, I'd like to see that hoodlum behind bars."

"Well, you can't blame her," Neil said. "I wish her all the luck in the world."

"You sound as though you meant that." Gram answered.

"Oh, I do!"

"Well, thank you, dear. I'll tell her."

When Gramps came in a few minutes later, he piled the boys in his car along with the sturdy old blue cushions that were now theirs, and drove them to Fish's.

"What are Jumbo cushions for?" Jamie wanted to

know, watching Fish and Neil carry them into the empty side of the garage.

"I'll fix 'em in place afterwards," Fish said to Neil. "Too late to practice now. Besides —" he pointed his chin in Jamie's direction.

"Right. We've got to go anyway. So long, Fish. It was a great thing your Gram did. Great."

"What are Jumbo cushions?" Jamie asked again, from the handlebars of Neil's bike as they rode home. "I wanna play Jumbo, too."

"It's no game," Neil said seriously. "It's hard, hard work. And I need it now like I never did before."

"Oh." Jamie lost interest in that. "Hey!" he exclaimed sliding to the ground in their driveway, "I'm going in and tell Mommy about Sarsaparilla!" He surged ahead and ran into the house. Neil headed for the toolshed with a thumping heart.

To him, it looked exactly as before. No recent signs of Trigger having changed a thing. The wisps of dry grass were trampled on and the scuffled film of talcum powder on the doorstep was only a dingy patch of gray. The same old newspapers blocked the dusty windowpanes. Although the brass doorknob turned easily in Neil's hand, the door was securely locked. He jiggled the knob and rapped on the glass. He could not hear a sound inside.

Got no chance of getting the key, he thought, as he studied the door, and not enough muscles to break it down, either, darn it. The door. What was familiar about that door? He tried hard to think. Suddenly it occurred to him. It was their old back door from the house, which had been remodeled a couple springs ago. Dad had taken their old back door and used it for the shed, replacing the tumbledown door it originally had. It could be unlocked from the inside. Just gotta bust a window, stick my hand inside and turn the button on the knob! So that part was cinchy.

Neil pressed his cheek against the cold windowpane. "Sarsaparilla?" he said softly. "Sarsaparilla, don't *you* give up the ship. Hear me? I'm gonna take you home. Soon as I can. Sarsaparilla?" He rattled the knob and then listened. Silence.

"Hope that stupid Trigger's been feeding you all right," he growled, turning away.

Rattle-Clunkety-Click!

"Good girl!" Neil roared. "Good old girl!"

He rushed into the house, got to the table cleaned up and on time for dinner and ate such a hearty meal that

Mother marveled at his appetite. She smiled. "Keep that up and we'll have a Hercules on our hands. With or without Judo."

That evening, alone in his room, Neil had to make up for lost time. He sat at his card table and cut out the sails for his *Mayflower* model. They were made of thin white plastic and he handled them as gingerly as eggshells, carefully taking tiny snips with Mother's manicure scissors so he wouldn't make a mistake. The only good thing about this dull job, he found out, was that it left his brain free to think about something else, mostly Hattie Atkins' Gingerbread House on Berkshire Road. That was on the other side of town out by the golf course. A good three miles and no short cuts that he knew of. There was no way he could carry Sarsaparilla, in her cage, in Trigger's big box, that far. No way. Besides, half the world would see him, maybe even Trigger himself, and Sarsaparilla, as everyone knew by now, was Stolen Property.

He put that unfinished idea aside and switched his thoughts to sorting out the sails. The littlest one is the sprit sail, he decided by consulting the diagram, and it goes to the fore. The largest one is the mainsail and it goes over the main topsail. This tapering lateen sail —

oh, baloney! Neil shoved his chair back and stood up stretching. He'd go see how Bonnie was doing for a change.

In the hall he could hear a few notes from her guitar and see a band of light under her door. "Anybody home?"

"Come on in, Neil," Bonnie was sitting in bed, her head bent over her guitar and her face half hidden by the long stream of hair shining in the light of her bedside lamp. Her blanket was strewn with school papers and pages from her looseleaf notebook. "These were on the floor," Neil said, picking up a fistful of random sheets.

"Thanks," Bonnie said, glancing at them. "Before I goofed off, I was trying to sort out my Nature Notebook for Mr. Lyon. It's almost due and all mixed up. Today didn't help." she glared at her heavy cast and flopped back against the pillows.

"This looks like kinda interesting stuff. 'Clues for a Twig Detective.' And this one on weeds — my gosh, they look like flowers. You do the drawings?"

Bonnie nodded. "Those are New England ones that blossom in the fall —"

"Hey, I've seen these in the woods lots of times.

'Joe-pye weed' it says. That's news to me."

"Oh, I can tell you about that. Joe Pye was an Indian medicine man. His tribe was sworn enemies with the early settlers in Massachusetts. Now this Joe Pye had a dog (on account of the wolves) and a little Puritan boy made friends with Joe Pye's dog, not knowing who it belonged to. They played together in the wilderness. One summer day when Joe Pye was out gathering herbs to make medicines with, he came upon them playing and that's how he and the boy got to know each other. They met lots of times in the woods. Then that fall, many of the settlers got sick with smallpox or typhus or something awful like that, and the little boy got it worst of all and he was dying. Now it seems Joe Pye had a secret cure he used for his own people, and when he heard about the little boy he badly wanted to help him because he was the only one who could."

"How'd he go about that?"

"Well, somehow he got through to the boy's parents, but they were afraid it was a trick. They thought Joe Pye would hurt their son instead of healing him. They didn't even believe he *knew* their son. In fact, the father got ready to shoot Joe Pye at the door with his gun. But Joe Pye said, 'I'll prove my story to you,' and he led his dog to the little boy's bedside, and the dog wagged and wagged his tail when he saw the boy. So the parents said, 'He must be telling the truth. He is a very brave man to come here.' And Joe Pye cured their son."

"Wow-ee," Neil said, half to himself, leaning against the maple bedpost. "Now there's a weed that amounted to something."

"You might say that." Bonnie nodded. "Anyway, that plant is named after him and it's still called joe-pye weed to this day in his honor."

"Well, I don't expect to become famous for it," Neil said gravely, "But I've got to pitch in there soon, come what may."

"Whatever that means," Bonnie replied.

Neil sauntered back to his room, took one look and let out a yowl that roused the household. He had caught a flash of Saucie in midair. She was leaping from the card table to the floor in guilty haste, leaving behind the overturned *Mayflower* model quivering on its side, paint jars knocked about and spools of rigging thread rolling off the table's edge. The ship's sails lay scattered on the hooked rug like flower petals. All that work gone to waste.

"What's happened?" Jamie asked, appearing in his pajamas.

"What is it?" Mother and Dad came charging up the stairs in alarm. Even Bonnie clumped out of her room on her crutches to see if she could help.

"Shipwrecked," Neil said in despair. He stood motionless by the card table while they picked up and put back to rights as much as they could. Jamie said, "Saucie's a baaaad girl."

Dad delicately replaced the *Mayflower* on its stand and fitted together the broken sheer-pole that would have to be mended with glue. Mother began to untangle the snarls in the rigging thread. Bonnie collected the featherweight sails in the palm of her hand.

"Much damage, would you say?" Dad asked.

"Oh, nothing that can't be fixed up, I guess," Neil answered. "I've just lost so much time, that's all." His eyes started to prickle.

"You've got tomorrow after school." Dad pointed out. "And the whole weekend with nothing planned."

With nothing planned! What do parents know

about *any*-thing, Neil wondered in exasperation. I've *got* to get Sarsaparilla back home *some*-how or other. And I've *got* to practice Judo with Fish before Trigger beats me up when he finds out. And Dad tells me I haven't got *any*-thing to do but slave over that blasted ship model.

"It takes so long for the paint to dry," Neil said irritably. He kicked his toe back and forth against the rung of the chair. "You can't put those drip-sized figures in place on the ship till they're painted and dry. And besides, I'm no artist."

"He ought to have some free time for play and fresh air," Mother put in. "There's also that Judo program on TV tomorrow night. And church on Sunday."

Dad heaved his shoulders. "Tell you what, Neil. Give it a try. Do as much as you can on the *Mayflower*, and I'll give the matter some further thought. I know you need that permission signature by Monday morning. I haven't forgotten that."

"Thanks, Dad."

By now Neil was ready and willing to go to bed. "Good night, sleep tight," he said, shoving Jamie out the door, the last one to leave. "Don't let the bedbugs bite."

6

Return Trip

FROM HIS OPEN WINDOW the next morning, very early, Neil peered out to see what kind of a day it was. New sunlight was sparkling on the grass, except for the precise quadrangle of frost, like a white paper cut-out, made by the shadow of the house. There was so little wind the leafless tree branches seemed like fossil designs on the stony sky. He sniffed the softened air. "Indian summer, almost." It was a good omen, and he felt a whoosh of hope.

About to turn, Neil sensed, rather than saw, a flicker of motion out of the corner of his eye. Holding his breath, he waited, fingers clutching the window sill and body held back so he couldn't be seen. Trigger! There was Trigger in his red windbreaker slipping out of the yard by the lilac bushes. Looking both ways when he reached the sidewalk, he veered to the left and broke into a run that whisked him out of sight. He was not carrying his big box with him.

There goes my last chance, Neil thought. Guess Trigger hasn't found the money yet. Anyway, he's not returning Sarsaparilla today. So I've got to. He had a plan, sort of a shaky one, but it was the best he could do alone and without someone to drive him in a car.

The minute the last bell rang at school that afternoon, Fish said, "See you at my house for Judo practice. Our gym's all set up and boy, are we ready to go!"

"Can't make it," Neil frowned. "Sorry, Fish. Tomorrow, I hope. Today I gotta plug away on a bunch of other stuff."

"Aw, you can do your model tonight, cantcha?"

"Well, there's that Judo show on TV tonight. Can't miss that."

"I s'pose not. But jeepers, Neil, I didn't think you'd back out now, after all that work."

"I'm *not* backing out. Tomorrow I'll be over. O.K.?" If I'm still alive, he added to himself. "O.K., Fish?"

"Oh, all right." He rubbed his nose against his knuckles and scowled. "It's no fun practicing Judo alone."

Neil didn't see how anyone could practice Judo alone, but he had his own problems and no time to lose. At home, one of the first things he did was to get Jamie's old cart out of the barn. Its wheels joggled and the handle was loose. Just hold together for one more trip, Neil begged, and try not to rattle so loud. He dragged it to the door of the toolshed and parked it next to his sleeping bag which he had left by the door. Now to find a good-sized rock. That was easy. There was a wide selection of them by the stone wall.

Next, he slid his right hand into one of Dad's canvas garden gloves, clutched the rock and raised his hand like a muscle-man. "Hang on to your hat, Sassy, I'm coming in!"

He drove the rock through the window with a splintering crash. Shards of jagged glass glinted in the sun, some still lodged in the putty of the window frame. He cleared the frame, stuck his hand inside and, brushing aside the flapping newspapers, turned the lock. He opened the door of the toolshed and cautiously stepped in.

Trigger had kept the light on, a shaded insect-repellent bulb that poured its cone of heated yellow light into the open corrugated carton that had been placed on the scarred wooden picnic table. A paper bag of birdseed and a soup can of water stood beside it. A trembling agitation of wings and feathers startled Neil as he looked into the box at a swirl of crayon-bright colors.

"Hello, Sarsaparilla, hello, girl. Take it easy, now." Behind the dull brass bars of the tall cage the parrot gradually subsided as Neil continued to make soothing little sounds to calm her. He saw that her head was yellow, her body and wings jungle green, with a swipe of red on her shoulders. Her eyes were sharp and her beak was hooked. Best of all, she was alive and kicking.

"*Rattle-Clunkety-Click!*" she snapped out at him in her cranky voice.

"You sure fooled me," Neil said. He wound his arms around the box, settled it on his hipbone for balance and slowly shuffled out of the shed, barely able to see where he was going.

"This is the first lap of your trip back home," he told her. He put the box on Jamie's cart and secured it with lengths of clothesline. "Be a good scout and pipe down. You won't like this much, it'll be dark and bumpy, but so long as you can breathe all right, don't complain to me." He covered the box with his unzipped sleeping bag and inspected his rig for take-off. After shutting the shed door, he started on his way, devoutly hoping no one would notice him.

"Hey Neil, where you going?" Jamie popped up from nowhere before Neil even got as far as Fish's house. (He was counting on Fish to be in his garage and safely out of sight.)

"None of your business. You go on home, Jamie."

"You got my cart. I want my cart."

"Well, I'm borrowing it. I'll give you my horseshoe magnet if you let me borrow it."

"I wanna go with you." He added cannily, "I could help, I betcha."

This was true, but Neil didn't dare risk it. "You go home. I mean it, Jamie."

Jamie, as a last resort, began to cry, small hiccoughing sobs that threatened to grow into full scale bellows.

"Button your lip! Don't you dare bawl your brains out or I'll tell Officer Kroznick on you. He can't stand babies. I've got to deliver this — this. Right now." Neil turned on his heel and marched down the sidewalk, the loaded cart rumbling after him. He refused to look back.

Not until he crossed the street at the second corner

did Neil sneak a glance in Jamie's direction. Jamie was sitting on the curb, his round chin lowered, his blond hair falling over his puckered brow. Although he wasn't going home, he wasn't following him, either. Whew!

Neil hauled the cart as far as the dentist's driveway without getting caught, run over or arrested. He was thinking ahead to the short cut in the woods and that narrow rocky path he would have to struggle through. He doubted the cart and box could make it without some snags. Maybe — Neil didn't see a plump lady in a mustard-colored coat coming out of Dr. Roberts' office until she fluttered her arm at him.

"Hello, there, Neil Applewhite!" It was Miss Mudgett, the third-grade teacher. She was pattering over to him, her fingers denting her puffy cheek. "My mouth's all numb," she said with a lopsided smile. "Dearie me, that's quite a cargo you're carrying there."

"Uh — yes —" Neil's voice trailed off. The sleeping bag was slipping to one side and he busied himself pulling it into place over the shoddy looking box. "I'm delivering a — a hand loom for my mother." Now what made him say a dumb thing like that! She hadn't even asked.

"Oh? To Dr. Roberts'?"

"No, no, not here. I'm going out back —" That didn't make sense, either — "I mean I'm — "

Rattle-Clunkety-Click!

Miss Mudgett twitched. "Heavens, what's that?"

"Ha, ha, ha," Neil laughed falsely. "This old wagon's full of crazy noises." He rattled the handle and jostled the wheels and said, "Sorry I have to rush away like this." He left her standing there with her unfinished conversation while he half-walked, half-ran into the woods, the box and cart hurtling after him. Boy, he thought, she's sure got me pegged Number-One Oddball. Again.

Alone in the woods, Neil folded up the sleeping bag and stuck it in back of the box. "You'll like that better," he told Sarsaparilla. "You can see the sky and make all the racket you want. Nobody's going to bother us during this stretch." The going was as rough as he had expected. It took skillful handling to keep the cart from tipping over and in some places he had to lift the wheels over gnarled roots and embedded stones. "Keep your cool, Sass. We're getting there." It was hot, hard work.

In one marshy spot their way was almost blocked by a thick clump of tall purple-pink flowers, nearly gone-by. They were stiff-stemmed with a few oval pointed leaves clinging like tatters. "Joe-pye weed!" Neil exclaimed. "Look at that, Sarsaparilla, a good luck sign if there ever was one." Excitedly he picked a small spray and wove it into the brass wires at the top of the cage. "That's so's you won't mind being covered up

again. We're almost to the field and I gotta put the sleeping bag back over the box."

Neil crossed the field and headed for Gram's brown-shingled house. There were no people around or any cars in sight. If only Gram's out shopping, he thought, or taking a nap or down cellar puttering about. Well, anyway, here we are. He left the cart by the steps and quietly went to the door of the side entry which Fish said was never locked. Cheers, it wasn't! He left the door ajar and went back for the big box. Still no one around. He dumped the sleeping bag on the ground and knelt down to untie the knotted clothesline. Only a few more minutes to go.

"For heaven's sakes, is that you, Neil?" Gram Fisher called out from the doorway.

Neil whirled to his feet and stood in front of the cart. Gram might be hard of hearing, but there was nothing wrong with her eyes behind those glittering granny glasses. "Oh. Hi. Hi, Gram Fisher," he called back.

"I felt a draft," she said. "And would you believe, this door was partway open. Otherwise, I might have missed you. Still getting things together for your Jumbo?" she asked, trying to get a better look.

"Got about everything now," Neil said, patting the box and swooping up the bag. "Just got to put this cover on." If Sassy made a fuss, at least the sound would be muffled. "On my way again," he announced, sorry that this was true.

"If there's anything I can do for you — ?" Gram asked, wondering why he'd stopped by.

"There is something. If you don't mind." Now that

his plan of leaving Sassy in Gram's side entry had back-fired, Neil was forced to think up a new plan on the spot. "Would you please call my mom and tell her I'll be late for dinner?" But not for that TV Judo show, if I can help it, he promised himself.

"Glad to, dear. I can see how well you might be! Don't you worry, I'll give her a ring right away."

"Thanks a heap." Neil left the yard, trundling the cart behind him, his passenger undelivered.

"We've already started this trip, Sassy," he told her. "So we might as well keep on going. It's nearer from here than from our house. No more toolshed for you. And no more stopovers, either. We'll do this by our-selves. You're going to get door-to-door service. How about that?"

No comment from Sarsaparilla.

Neil squared his shoulders and trudged the length of Oak Street until he came to the crossroads. Bearing left, he took the golf course road where the sidewalks ended and the houses were few. Although he had often ridden out this way on his bicycle, he'd never noticed before how bumpy and hilly and curvy it was, espe-cially for a rickety cart with a big box on top. Twice he had to retie the ropes and tuck in the cover. A couple cars passed him and once a fat raccoon crossed the road in front of him. The sky was beginning to darken and the air smelled wetly of brooks and pine needles.

Both arms and the backs of his legs felt tired by the time Neil wound his way up Berkshire Road. Catching sight of Hattie Atkins' old ark looming at the end of the rutted drive, Neil dropped the handle of the cart, stopping by the entranceway made of cemented stones.

"There's home, sweet home, at last, Sassy," he said, removing the sleeping bag for good and looking down at her spiky yellow head. She eyed him sullenly. No thanks for that lurchy, pitching ride. "Cheer up," he said. "All we have to do now is think of how to get you in that place and me out." I've got to keep her in the box, he thought, so she won't catch cold. 'Cause I'll have to leave her outside. On the veranda — I guess that's the best bet — if I don't get caught. No lights on and no sign of that Model T. Maybe nobody's home (let's hope). Or else it's parked in that falling-down building under the trees. I can't tell. Anyhow, here goes!

Neil followed the drive to the cavernous front entrance. Dusk blurred his vision like a smudge of charcoal and the bulk of the box made it hard to move without stumbling. Overgrown hedges smothered the front steps and fancy railings. The top stair creaked beneath his foot and there was a sudden *Rattle-Clunkety-Click!* from Sassy.

"Stop right there!" commanded a shrill new voice.

Neil dropped the box with a thud. He blinked his eyes to see a frantic brown-branchy figure in a frayed sweater and hitched-up skirt hopping up and down in front of him. She was no taller than he was.

"That's my Sarsaparilla! I know it is. Oh, let me have her. Please! Please! Here's your ransom money. Take it!" she flung an envelope at Neil who tried to push it away.

"No, no!" he blurted out. "I didn't come for that. I only — "

The envelope fell between them. Hattie Atkins lifted the brass cage out of the box and wrapped her arms around it, holding it tightly to her chest. Sassy was flapping her wings against the bars and screeching, "Ship ahoy! Ship ahoy!"

"I never heard her say *that* before," Neil said.

"She just says it when she's overexcited." She set the cage down gently and blew the unruly hair from her forehead. "Alive and well. I can scarcely believe it."

Noticing the sprig of joe-pye weed stuck through the top, she pulled it out and held it closely to her button-bright eyes, studying the leaves and nodding to herself. "So Sarsaparilla was hidden in the woods."

"No, not there — she had better care than that. Honest."

"Well, I should hope so. She's a Panama Amazon and deserves the best. Belonged to my eldest brother and better company than a number of people I could name. You can't *imagine* how dreadful it was to be without her." A quiver of pain flickered over her small walnut-shell face.

"Oh yes I can!" Neil said. "Our dog Gypsy got run over and I — I miss her all the time. I know what it's like."

Hattie Atkins scrutinized Neil in the semi-darkness.

"You're not the same person who called me up, are you?"

"No, I'm not him. I only came to bring Sassy back."

"That other one — I presume he sent you here."

"Nobody sent me here, Mrs. Atkins. I came by myself. I found out where Sassy was and I got her out and I brought her home. I *was* going to leave her at Gram Fisher's house but — "

"A likely story! You're not fooling me. That other one — no doubt he's lurking in the shrubbery this very minute, waiting for you to give him the ransom. Ye gods and little fishes, where is it?" She started to scrounge around on the floor. Neil felt obliged to help her. He slid the big box over by the weathered wicker chairs and tables that huddled in groups on the deserted veranda and he pushed aside the collection of pots and jars haphazardly stacked by the doorway.

"The ransom's all in that envelope, fifteen one-dollar bills. I counted them out myself," Hattie Atkins sputtered as she swept her spidery hands along the paint-peeled floor boards. "Oh botheration. I just had it with me a while ago. Thought you'd never show up. Can't think why it took you so long to come collect it."

Neil, also on his hands and knees, nearly backed into Sassy's cage. For once, Sassy seemed to be enjoying herself. "But I didn't come for the ransom, Mrs. Atkins," Neil insisted. "That's not the reason — "

"Here it is!" Hattie Atkins cried. She caught Neil off balance as he was getting to his feet and stuffed the thick brown envelope into his jacket pocket. "Now be off with you," she said, giving him a rap on the shoulder blades that started him down the steps. "No

more mischief from you or your cohorts — you hear?"

Neil didn't know what a cohort was nor how to explain that she'd gotten everything all mixed up. "I wish I could — "

"Never mind," she said. "Just go along. You've caused me enough trouble already." She stood her ground at the top of the stairs with Sarsaparilla at her side.

He kept on going. She couldn't listen to me anyway. I've got a pocketful of ransom by mistake, he thought, but I can't prove it, not to her. At the stone entranceway he rolled up the sleeping bag and put it in the empty cart. A sudden chill shot him full of duck bumps — wait till Trigger finds out Sassy's gone and so is the money! He'll be out to get me for sure.

Neil picked up the handle, bent his head and started running, the cart rattling after him like hailstones on the road. He had a long way to go and he had to hurry. Couldn't miss that TV Judo show, especially not now. He needed all the pointers he could get.

7

The Ransom by Mistake

Lucky for you we had chicken pie and peas tonight," Bonnie said. "That keeps." The family was eating dessert by the time Neil got home, rumpled and sweaty and starving to death.

"There's tossed salad, too," Mother said. "Your plate's in the kitchen."

"May I eat out there?" Neil asked. He could gulp it down faster with nobody to mind and also keep his eye on the clock.

"Certainly," Mother said. "And thank you for having Gram Fisher give me a call."

"But we weren't worried," Dad admitted. "We knew you'd show up tonight of all nights. For your Judo program. Told some fellows at the office about it and they're going to watch it, too."

"So's Cappy," Neil called back, piling his plate high with chunks of chicken and skipping the peas. "I mean Mr. Capaccio. And so's Fish and his folks."

"And so's *us*," Jamie said, his mouth full of rice pudding with raisins. "When does it start?"

"Six-thirty," Bonnie answered. "Even I've heard enough by now to know that."

By 6:25 Neil had herded everyone into the family room to watch the Friday edition of "Sports Highlights." Jamie switched the dial to the local channel and sat cross-legged on the floor in front of the brightening blue screen. He wasn't mad at Neil anymore because the horseshoe magnet was more fun than marbles. He reached over and parked it on the buckle of Mother's shoe. She was sitting on the couch hemming Mrs. Wyman's napkins and Dad was next to her sorting out the evening paper.

"This better be good," Bonnie said from the depths of her armchair, her legs resting on the leather footstool. Saucie was asleep in her lap, curled up like a seashell. "We're missing a super mystery on channel four."

"It's gonna be the greatest," Neil predicted. He couldn't stand still, prowling from one place to another, wishing the Saltines commercial would hurry up and finish so the real show could start. "Hey, this is it!"

The good-natured face of the sportscaster beamed at

them in an orange glow as he welcomed his fans to " —
a special treat. Before introducing tonight's distin-
guished guest, let me whet your appetite with this brief
display of skill."

The camera focused on two teen-aged boys dressed
in traditional white Judo outfits. They bowed to each
other and then flew into separate whirls of motion like
paper pinwheels on a windy day. One fell backward,
rolled and landed on the mat with a loud slap of his
hand and forearm. The other plummeted forward,
landing on his right shoulder with equal grace. They
sprang to their feet and bowed again.

The camera returned to the sportscaster and his
slight dark-haired guest. "Friends, meet Dick Grodin,
an ex-Marine, Brown Belt holder and at present Judo
Instructor at the Salisbury YMCA. Dick, won't you
please tell our viewing audience about the ancient art of
self-defense without weapons — in other words, Judo."

"Gladly." The soft-spoken man had a lean hard
face. "First of all, what you just saw was a typical
warm-up exercise. The boys will demonstrate a throw,
called the Floating Drop, later on in the program.
Judo, may I explain, translated from the Japanese,
means, 'the gentle way.' "

Neil snuck a glance at Mother. She really looked surprised.

"Its traditions," Brown Belt Dick Grodin continued, "come from the Samurai, or warrior, class of feudal Japan and a weaponless manner of self-defense called Jujitsu. In the late nineteenth century, Professor Jigaro Kano, a master of the martial arts, refined Jujitsu into a tremendous sport. He eliminated everything harmful. The objective of Judo is to cultivate mind and body to the fullest extent, developing willpower and discipline as well as physical fitness. President Theodore Roosevelt was one of the first Americans to excel in this sport."

This time Dad looked more impressed than the sportscaster, who probably already knew these enlightening historical facts.

The sportscaster asked, "Do you recommend Judo for boys, say from nine or ten on up?"

"Telephone's ringing!" Jamie said, scrambling to his feet. "I'll get it." He ran into the kitchen before Neil could finish saying, "Wouldntcha know! If it's for me, I'll call back later."

"It's probably Janie," Bonnie said. "She —"

"Sh — sh — " Neil said, not wanting Mom and Dad

to be distracted. Yes, it seemed Dick Grodin did heartily recommend Judo for boys —

"Neil," Jamie whispered, pinching at his sleeve. "It's somebody who sounds mad at you. Awful mad. You better go."

With a howl of protest, Neil tore his eyes away from the Judo expert and forced himself to leave. Why would anybody in his right mind make a phone call in the middle of the best show, no matter how mad he was? "If you're kidding me, Jamie —" He went into the dark kitchen and picked up the receiver. "Hello," he said. "Neil Applewhite speaking."

"Listen, I just got home from that toolshed in your backyard and it's been broke into. The window's busted and my box is gone. I wanna know what happened." Neil winced at Trigger's loud voice like static in his ear.

"You said for me to stay clear of that place. You said —"

"Don't tell me what I said, stinkweed. I'm asking you what happened to my box. There was something important inside it. And someone was going to pay me a lot of dough to get it back."

"Nobody told me what was inside it."

"I'll tell ya. In case you seen it somewhere. It was a bird."

"A bird?"

"Yeah, some kind of pet parrot. Now it didn't fly off by itself, any goof knows that. It's in a cage. And it's gotta be fed and took care of, if it's gonna stay alive. Whattaya think I been doing every day?"

"I don't know."

"Oh, you don't know from nothin'." Trigger sounded disgusted and discouraged. "I gotta get holda that parrot. To get my money at the Atkins' place. Something fishy's going on and if you're at the bottom of it, I'll find out. I got ways. Next time I talk to you it won't be on the phone." He hung up.

Neil replaced the receiver. His hand hurt from holding it so tightly. He felt the lump of the brown envelope wadded into his pants pocket where he had put it for safe keeping. It gave him a crawly feeling in the pit of his stomach to know how badly Trigger wanted it. He could hardly wait till later tonight when, in the privacy of his own room, he could spread out the bills on his bed and count them and decide what he ought to do with them. What a headache it was to be in charge of all this ransom that wasn't his!

"Who was it?" Bonnie asked when Neil returned to the family room.

"Oh, just some guy from school. Didn't know beans about the Judo show."

"He was a dope," Jamie dismissed him cheerily. "You missed the Floating Drop, Neil," he added, doing a backward somersault. "I wish I could do it."

"Me, too," Neil said bleakly. The sportscaster was winding up the show saying, " — Beginner's Class for boys nine to thirteen — formed at the Y — final registration date, Monday, November fifteenth."

"Sounds like a winner," Dad said. "You were absolutely right, Neil. That Judo class would be a natural for you."

"All I need is your signature."

"And the *Mayflower?*"

"Still plugging away."

"We got a surprise for you," Jamie said. "Can I tell him now? Can I?" Bonnie dimpled, watching Neil with sparkly eyes and closed lips.

"First let me say this," Mother interrupted. "After what we saw tonight on TV, I'm really delighted you want to join that Judo class they're starting. I was apprehensive in the beginning, but I'm not any more. At least not so much."

"I'm all for it, too," Dad said. "Always have been. Which brings us up to our bargain, Neil. You only have till Monday morning to finish your model and time's running out. That shipwreck of Saucie's cost you hours of work and it wasn't your fault. Before you got home, we had a family conference. Bonnie's idea, really — and we approve wholeheartedly."

"What is it?" Neil asked.

"You'll see," Jamie promised. "Come on, Neil. I'll show you." He dragged Neil by the hand and pulled him upstairs. Bonnie followed after them, lugging her crutches and hobbling up one step at a time. Jamie opened the door to Neil's room and switched on the light.

"Surprise!" Bonnie chirped, sitting down in Neil's chair at the card table and picking up a paintbrush. "I'm painting the little Pilgrim people for your model," she announced. "Oh, Neil, it's such fun and I love doing it. Dad said it was O.K. D'you mind?"

"Heck, no! Be my guest." This was good luck if he ever saw it. He bent down to inspect Governor William Bradford. Bonnie had painted his helmet silver and his ankle-length cloak a brilliant red. "He looks terrific. Where's Myles Standish?"

"The Captain?" Bonnie asked, as she searched for him. "He's this one. I'm doing him like the other Pilgrim Fathers. Gray tunic with white collar and cuffs. Black hat and boots. They're still wet, so don't touch. Like him?"

"You bet I do."

"I like this little Pilgrim boy," Jamie said, poking a finger at him. "Do him next."

"Well, I can't do everything at once," Bonnie said, shaking back her hair. "I want to do lots more tomorrow. I got so sick of hanging around with this stupid old cast."

"About ready to close up shop for the night?" Neil asked. Glad as he was to have Bonnie's help, he wished she could carry on somewhere else. The ransom was a thorn in his pocket.

"Oh, I'll do a few more people," she said, getting settled. "I'm dying to get to Oceanus Hopkins in her tiny little cradle, but I'm saving her till last. I'm not the least bit tired and there's this neat disk jockey to listen to. Turn on the radio, huh, Jamie? We don't have to go to bed early Friday nights, anyway."

"No school tomorrow," Jamie chanted. "No school tomorrow." He was trying out Bonnie's crutches without much success. "Can I paint too?"

"Thanks, but don't bother," Neil said. "And no visits to my room unless Bonnie says. Hey, look — there's Saucie! Grab her, Jamie. I don't want *her* in here again. She's hiding under the bed."

Jamie crawled under the bed and hauled out the protesting Applesauce. "She just wants to see what's going on — don't you, Saucie?" Jamie carried her away with him downstairs, burying his nose in her furry neck and telling her, "Don't mind them, they're no fun."

There wasn't room at the card table for two to be working at once. Neil lounged around, trying to act busy for what seemed like hours. At last Bonnie decided she'd had enough. Unlike him, she was so neat it took her a long time to clean up the brushes and put the table back in order.

"Thanks a whole lot," Neil said when she stood up. He got her crutches for her. "See you in the morning." Wow! Now he could close the door for good and get out the ransom money.

With shaky fingers, he pried the brown envelope out of his pants pocket and unstuck the flap. The wad of money was bound by a wide elastic. Hurriedly he smoothed the wrinkles from his bedspread to make a flat place where he could lay out the fifteen one-dollar bills. Some were old and some were new and they marched in a line to his pillow. He had never seen so many at once. And he had no idea what to do about them.

That night Neil went to bed with the thick brown envelope, full of the money, under his pillow. It was a hard lump that didn't make his head feel good outside when he lay on it or inside when he thought about it. Even if all those bills belonged to him personally, just pretend, they couldn't buy him one thing he wanted badly. What he wanted most was to have lots of muscles and to be a couple feet taller. Next to that, he wanted to be a Judo champ and the money didn't have any power over that, either. It couldn't even get the *Mayflower* finished or Dad's signature on the registration card. He couldn't spend it and he couldn't keep it around, either. But how was he going to get rid of it? He wouldn't be so nutty as to bury it and he couldn't very well dump it in the collection basket at church on

Sunday without somebody noticing and asking a million questions.

Hattie Atkins thought he had to give it to "That Other One," meaning Trigger. Well, why not really give it to Trigger? She had her parrot back and Trigger would have his money and I'd have Trigger off my back once and for all. It was an easy way out and no grown-up would be any the wiser. Why not?

Neil sat bolt upright in bed. I'll be gosh-darned if I'll hand that ransom over to Trigger. No sir, not me! Besides, he doesn't even know I've got it. He lay back on his pillow. I don't know what I'll do with it, he thought, but at least I know all the things I *won't* do with it.

Early the next morning, before anyone was awake, Neil dressed warmly and went out to the toolshed to clean up the remains of Sassy's stay. The brown envelope was once again stashed in his pants' pocket. He threw away the soup can and the paper bag of birdseed, and he made sure no pieces of glass were left around. So far as he knew, Dad hadn't noticed the broken window.

The sky above the treetops blazed with the rising sun and two squirrels chased each other across the field and over the stone wall. If only I can keep out of Trigger's way, Neil thought, breathing deep and swinging his arms in circles, at least till I'm a whiz at Judo.

"Neil! Whatcha doing, Neil?" Jamie's blond head stuck out of his upstairs bedroom window.

"Picking dandelions," Neil shouted back. "What does it look like?"

"I dunno. Mom's making pancakes for breakfast. Come on in." Neil didn't need a second invitation.

As the family was finishing breakfast, they heard a loud pounding at the back door. Neil's heart skipped a beat. Would Trigger come barging in to get him?

"It's Fish," Jamie yelled. "Oh, wait till you see!"

"I'll take my jacket off first," Fish called from the back hall. "Can't hardly wait to show you."

Everyone at the kitchen table looked up to watch Fish make his entrance. He strutted in like a plump white rooster, his face red with pleasure.

"Wowee! Oh, wowee," Neil breathed.

"This is my *gi*," Fish said. He was wearing a brand-new Judo suit. Made of strong white material, the top was tied around his waist with a long white belt. The roomy white pants came just below his knees. "My mother made me wear shoes and socks," he apologized.

"It's really keen-looking without them."

"It's keen-looking, anyhow," Jamie said, walking around him to get a full view.

"The sleeves are s'posed to be loose like this," Fish said, waggling his wrists.

"Regulation all the way," Dad said.

"And my fingernails are cut short," Fish added, holding out his splayed hands for them to check. "Gotta keep 'em that way so's you don't scratch your partner. And I don't have any rings on or any metal objects, neither. That's regulations, too."

"This is the first in-person Judo suit I've ever seen," Bonnie said.

"Me, too," Neil and Jamie echoed.

"You look mighty handsome, Fish," Mother said. "I know you'll do well." Fish lowered his eyelashes and blushed.

"Where'd you get it?" Neil wanted to know.

"My Mom ordered it and it just came this morning, parcel post. When you're done eating, let's get in some practice. How about it?"

"Will if I can. Gotta put something away first."

Fish's face fell. "You're always busy lately. What's going on?"

"Be right back," Neil said and ducked out to his bedroom. After weighty consideration, he hid the brown envelope full of the ransom money in his pillowcase. Then he made his bed with care. It looked much better than usual.

"O.K., Fish, let's go." Fish was sitting at the round pine table eating pancakes drenched with maple syrup from their own trees. Sunlight filled the kitchen and the bright blue sky of autumn was reflected in the window panes. "In just a sec. Jeepers, is this ever good, Mrs. Applewhite."

On their way over to Fish's garage, Fish said, "Let's not rough it up too much — 'cause, gosh, if I ripped this suit — I mean *gi* — I'd be in some pickle." He patted his top protectively. "To tell you the truth, Neil, I don't even want to get it *dirty*. I never felt like *that* before."

"Don't blame you. It'll be different at the Y when we're all alike. Why don't you put on your jeans like me? For now, I mean."

"Right. Boy, oh boy, this is finally going to be our first real practice, isn't it? We've got our own private gym —"

"And our own special gym mats —"

"And some warm-ups we can try out like on TV. You know," Fish went on, "seriously. That show was so fantastic last night, we oughta write a letter and mail it to the TV station."

"*That's it!*" Neil yowled, whanging his knee with the flat of his hand. Oh so simple, the perfect solution. Like a flashbulb going off in his head.

"I know it's a good idea," Fish said modestly. "But you don't have to go off your rocker over it."

"Hey, Fish," Neil said urgently. "I gotta go home. I just thought of something I gotta do. I'll tell you later." Fish's popped-open eyes made him feel like a skunk, but he couldn't help it. "See you." He turned and ran.

"Not — not if I see you first, Neil Applewhite," Fish shouted in a choked-up voice. "You — you fake friend!"

Neil couldn't answer. He ran home and up to his room with a thumping heart. Luckily Bonnie was talking to Janie on the phone and hadn't started to work painting *Mayflower* Pilgrims. He was alone. He shut the door and dug out the ransom money from inside his pillowcase, forgetting to remake the bed. He counted the fifteen bills one last time, wound the elastic around them and put them in the worn brown envelope. Then he got his ballpoint pen and sat down at the card table.

In neat block letters he printed on the front:

TO MRS. HATTIE ATKINS
BERKSHIRE ROAD
HAWTHORNE, MASS.

PRIVATE! PERSONAL! PRIVATE!

He helped himself to five eight-cent stamps (better to have plenty) from the desk in the family room. Noticing that they were Wildlife Conservation stamps, he chose the ones that pictured a Brown Pelican because that was sort of in honor of Sarsaparilla. He licked them well and pounded them on to make sure that they would stick. With Scotch tape, he sealed up the flap. There.

Grasping the envelope tightly, Neil wheeled his bike from the barn and peddled up the street, headed for the nearest mailbox. It was in the general direction of Trigger's house and Neil fervently hoped Trigger didn't have to work for Potter's Market this morning. This was the way he would have to go.

No such luck. He caught sight of Trigger's red windbreaker at the same moment Trigger turned his head and spotted him. No one else was around.

"Looking for me?" Trigger asked, hulking toward

him in his heavy boots. Neil swerved his bike around and tried to get away. Of all the rotten breaks, this was the worst.

"Not so fast, stinkweed." Trigger sprinted after him, kicking at the back wheel as though it were a football. The bike tipped over on the pavement and Neil went with it. He squeezed his eyes shut and shook his head to clear the dizziness. His hands and knees were scraped and stinging.

Trigger loomed over him. "What's this?" he asked, making a grab for the brown envelope that Neil had somehow continued to clutch. His cramped fingers gave out and Trigger had it with his second try. Examining his prize with growing disbelief, Trigger finally gave a long low whistle. "It's the ransom," he muttered, pressing his fingers against the thick wad and rereading Hattie Atkins' name.

Neil dragged himself to the curb and sat down, his head in his hands.

Slowly a dumbfounded smile spread over Trigger's face. He sat on the curb beside Neil.

"I gotta hand it to you, kid," he said. "I told you about the old lady's parrot and you went right over and picked up the ransom for yourself. Can't figure out

how you found it. I musta looked in that flower-pot thing by her back door about sixteen times. Always empty, by George. Thought she hadn't heard me right, but every time I called her up, her line was busy. Guess we'll never know what became of the bird. Who cares? I got the money."

"What do you want the money for, anyway?" Neil asked grumpily. "You have a job."

"I'll tell ya. My folks bank the money I make and all I get is a dinky allowance. Peanuts. Ya know what I want? A pair of Bobby Orr hockey skates. Thirteen dollars and ninety-nine cents at the Salisbury Discount. Zowie! I'm gonna hitch over there this after and buy 'em. Right now, I'm late for Potter's. See ya around."

Trigger swaggered down the sidewalk. "Oh, I forgot," he said with a smirk. "Here's your key to the toolshed." He tossed it toward Neil. "I won't be needing that no more."

8

Joe-Pye Weed

NEIL PICKED UP the toolshed key. He didn't hurt too much and his bike wasn't damaged beyond a dent in the back fender. Slowly he coasted home, his brains a blank. He put away his bike in the barn and hung up the key on the nail. No one knew it had ever been missing. He wandered about the yard slinging a few stones across the field. He found a crooked stick under one of the pear trees and peeled off the bark. With the tip he scraped his initials in the hardened dirt path. He wondered what to do. Fish was mad at him and he couldn't think of a good reason to call him up and make friends. Their Judo practice was at a standstill before it ever got started. If only he had Gypsy. Gypsy always wanted to be with him no matter what. Not like Applesauce. She was fun to have around (most of the time) but she did as she pleased and it wasn't the same.

Mother came out of the house with Jamie. "Why so down in the mouth?" she asked. "We're going to

Salisbury to do some shopping. Want to come?"

"No thanks," Neil said. "I was just going in to work on the *Mayflower*. Time's about up."

"Dragging your heels," Mother said, shaking her head. "That didn't turn out to be your favorite hobby, did it?"

"It's Bonnie's favorite hobby, I betcha," Jamie said. "She does it real good. Let's go, Mom." He pulled at her coat. "Bye, Neil."

Neil waved good-by and went in to see Bonnie. She was busy at the card table in his room and he could tell before she spoke that she was doing a fantastic job. "Look at these," she said proudly, leaning forward and showing him the curving plastic sails. "It was my own idea to antique them. I rubbed yellow chalk around the edges and highlighted the middle with white." They looked old and mellow and just right for the timbered ship.

"I never would have thought of that," Neil said. "They're better 'n the sails on the model we saw in the souvenir shop."

"Next I'm going to make the nameplate. It's a separate little stand that says *Mayflower* on it in fancy old English letters. I'm going to paint the letters gold and the background blue. You better patch up the mizzen mast, though, if we're going to get this thing done on time."

"I guess I'd better." He flopped on the side of his bed and yawned. Somehow that model made him tired every time he looked at it. Only the thought of getting Dad's signature on the Judo registration card could spur him into action. Ho-hum. Up and at 'em.

"The telephone's ringing!" Bonnie said. "You get it, Neil. It takes me forever with this cast."

As usual, it was for Bonnie. "It's a boy. Wants to speak to you." Neil reported. "Don't know who it is."

He was dawdling over the next-to-last page of the directions when Bonnie came bobbing back. Her cheeks were pink and she kept brushing away her long hair with excited little flicks. "Guess who," she breathed, sinking into the desk chair. Neil shrugged. "The frog boy! That boy from the third-period class who had the frog. He was only trying to show it to me when it jumped out of his hands by mistake. He didn't mean to scare me and he felt awful about it and he wants me to know he's sorry. He found out from Janie I'm in a cast, but I said that's nothing, I can go back to school Monday."

"You sound like you can't wait."

"I don't have to," she giggled. "He's coming over tomorrow around four. To help me with my Science Notebook. It's a mess. His name is Scott Dunlevy. Says his sister Janet's in your room at school."

"Calamity J.? That's what Cappy calls her 'cause she's always in a jam. Sure I know her. She's a good kid. Did your friend Scott get it for pitching you in the ditch?"

"He *didn't* pitch me in any ditch. I fell by myself. But Mr. Lyon gave him detention anyway. Too bad, huh?"

"Well, now that your interest in Science has been revived, I s'pose that means you won't have any more time for this junk."

"Don't be silly. I like doing this. Honest. But I've got to wash my hair pretty soon. And decide what clothes to wear and all. Prob'ly my long calico skirt. Look, these sails are done — you figure out where they go and how to hitch them on."

Between them, with various interruptions, snacks and time off for TV, not counting Sunday morning at church and the family dinner afterwards, they finished the *Mayflower* by quarter of three Sunday afternoon, except for a couple Pilgrim Fathers who weren't dry enough to glue onto the deck.

"I got a good idea," Neil said. "Let's put this ship on the mantle in the family room right now. We can stick those Fathers on later."

"Sure thing," Bonnie agreed. "But you'll have to carry it down. And be *careful!*"

"You bet I will. Gee, thanks a million, Bonnie. I'd've been sunk without you."

"That's O.K. Come on. I'm dying to see how it looks — at a distance."

Neil cleared the mantle except for a pair of brass candlesticks at one end and the shelf clock at the other. He placed the *Mayflower* squarely in the middle. Bonnie called Mother and Dad to "Come on in to see a Believe-It-or-Not."

"Beautiful," Mother said. "A masterpiece."

"Happy landings." Dad beamed. "A job well done. With a little help from your friend."

"With lotsa help," Neil said. "Now then, Dad, how's about signing me up for Judo? I got the registration card right here and a pen in my pocket."

"My pleasure, son. Get — "

"Neil! Mommy, Daddy!" Jamie shouted, running

into the room at the speed of a spinning top. "That funny old shiny old car — the one you saw at Gram Fisher's — I just saw it! It's coming up our street. Come see!"

All except Neil followed Jamie to the living room windows to see this antique wonder on wheels. Neil stood stiffly where he was by the fireplace, hoping the car would drive right by. He had a hunch it wouldn't. A few minutes later he heard the front doorbell ring, a single long peal. That would be Hattie Atkins. He didn't know how she found out who he was, but what did it matter. She wouldn't believe a word he said.

"You have a visitor," Mother said to Neil, coming into the family room with a puzzled expression. She patted the hair down at the back of his head and straightened the collar of his jersey. "She's very anxious to see you, dear. Privately."

Neil stood up, drew in a deep breath and walked slowly toward the living room. He passed by Bonnie and Dad, tugging the gaping Jamie along between them, as they retreated into the family room. At first he hardly recognized the small figure sitting in the wing chair. A pleated black silk hat rose like a crown on top of her head and scrolly gold earrings swung from her earlobes. Gold chains, lockets, and cameos gleamed against her lace front, and the folds of her black skirt nearly reached her ankles. She sat bolt upright and her black satin shoes pointed straight ahead. A large lumpy tapestried knitting bag was planted by her feet.

"I'm glad to see you, Neil Applewhite," she said at

once in her husky voice. "Bring up a chair and sit next to me, so we can talk."

Neil moved the bannister chair to her side and sat down, hands clutching the seat and heels notched on the rung. "How are you, Mrs. Atkins?"

"Full of information that will interest you," she answered. She raised her chin and peeled off her white kid gloves one finger at a time.

Neil felt a flutter of panic. "What's that?" he asked as politely as possible.

"The last time I saw you," she said, "I leaped to a number of conclusions. Mistaken ones, I grant you. I was barking up the wrong tree. I admit it. That's a failing of mine and I make no excuses. Delirious as I was to have my Sarsaparilla back home, afterward I couldn't help feeling uneasy about your part in her disappearance — or, I should say, her reappearance. I recalled that somewhere along the line you mentioned Gram Fisher's name. So I discussed my perplexity with her. I told her exactly what had happened as best I could relate it and from my description, she knew immediately who you were."

Neil shifted uncomfortably.

" 'That's Neil Applewhite to a T,' she said, 'a fine boy. My grandson's best friend, to boot.' And sure enough, as proof of the pudding, she said you *had* been in her yard with the big box on Friday. (Though at the time she had no idea what was in it!) What you had said about acting on your own began to ring true, though I did not know the circumstances. As a matter of fact, I was glad I'd made you take the ransom money because to my mind you deserved it."

"I didn't want — " Neil began.

Hattie Atkins held up her hand. She had all the command of Officer Kroznick. "There's more," she said. "Something astounding happened that opened my eyes still wider. You are the only person I plan to tell. The whole story, anyway. That's between the two of us. Part of it I'll have to tell your parents and you'll see why later on."

Neil's scalp prickled. What plan could she have up her sleeve now?

"Bear with me," she said. "Yesterday morning around eleven I was in the kitchen mixing up a batch of bran muffins. My order from Potter's Market arrived, delivered by that great oaf of a boy, Trigger Deal. He never says a word, aye, yes or no, unless I force it out of him, so I usually just say, 'Put them there, please.' I was about to do so when all of a sudden Sarsaparilla started ruffling her feathers and flapping her wings and making those new *clunkety-click* sounds — oh, she was in a tizzy! That Deal boy nearly dropped to the floor at the commotion. That's when it struck me like a clap of thunder. I put two and two together." Her dark eyes glittered. "So idiotic of me not to catch on sooner."

Neil dug his nails into his palms. She was on the right track, all right.

"That day, last Tuesday, when I had my open house for Nellie Nugent, I had some groceries sent in. Not my refreshments — they were all prepared — just my regular order, which is why I didn't give it a second thought. And here I was calling up thirty to thirty-five guests of mine, searching for clues to Sarsaparilla's disappearance, when that culprit had gone in and out of my back door without the slightest suspicion. He had never, to my knowledge, paid the least bit of attention to my parrot. I don't trust a person without any natural feelings toward a pet. Indeed I don't." Her lips were puckered in a stern line like a thread drawn too tight.

" 'Well now,' I said to that Trigger as cool as a cucumber. 'I'd say Sarsaparilla was telling me something, Wouldn't you?' He went red as a beet. But he's a fresh one. 'I see you got your bird back,' he muttered. 'So you got your money's worth.' I started to laugh." She cackled to herself remembering. "Heaven knows what prompted me. I said, 'That's *marked* money. Anybody caught passing those bills anywhere in these United States will be in a peck of trouble with the authorities. A peck of trouble.' "

"Marked money!" Neil nearly slid out of his chair.

"Not really. I must have picked up the notion on television."

"What did Trigger do?"

"The most astonishing thing. He huffed, and puffed, and shuffled his feet, and fumbled in his jacket pocket. He was mighty frightened, let me tell you."

Trigger Deal, frightened by this scrap of an old lady who didn't have a muscle to her name!

"At last Trigger said to me, 'Mrs. Atkins, I know the little squirt who had your bird hid in his toolshed. Neil Applewhite, maybe you know him. I made him fork over that ransom money to me this morning — so I could give it back to you. Didn't know it was marked bills, neither.' And would you believe it, he shoved that brown envelope full of the ransom money into my hands as though it was a lighted firecracker. I saw that it had been addressed to me. Obviously, you'd been about to mail it back when he overtook you."

Neil shut his eyes. She knew everything.

"Trigger can't afford the kind of trouble I could cause him and he knows it. Actually, I don't want him to lose his job if he's learned his lesson. I know he won't try any more hocus-pocus with *me*. From now on, I can keep tabs on him in my own way, maybe even shift his direction a whisker. We'll see." She pursed her mouth. "The mystery to me," she said, "is why didn't Trigger find that money for himself in one of those flower pots."

"He told me he looked in 'a flower-pot thing' by your back door about sixteen times."

"A flower-pot thing — oh, oh! He must have meant my old porcelain *umbrella* stand!"

She laughed till her eyes watered and so did Neil. "Trigger sure is dumb for a guy who was going to outwit *us!*" he said.

Hattie Atkins laid her hand lightly on Neil's. "I'm grateful for that 'us,' " she said. "I realize beyond measure how much trouble and peril you went through for the sake of Sarsaparilla and her well-being. You're full of spunk, Neil Applewhite."

"Well," Neil said dubiously. "I don't know. Most of the time, I was pretty scared."

"Young man," Hattie Atkins said severely, "without fear there *is* no courage. This roundabout ransom has proven that. Now go get your family. I have a presentation to make."

Neil rounded up Mother and Dad, Jamie and Bonnie. They trooped into the living room and sat down after the introductions were made. All faces were turned toward Hattie Atkins in the wing chair. She cleared her throat and tucked a wisp of hair under her crown-like hat.

"It gives me much pleasure to tell you this," she said formally. "This past week, as you may have heard, my beloved parrot Sarsaparilla disappeared from my home. Neil, all alone and at great risk to himself, assumed the responsibility of returning her to me. The details don't matter. Suffice to say, I am deeply indebted to his sound heart and sturdy backbone. You may well be proud of him. I hope he will accept, therefore, this small token — "

She bent down and opened the large tapestry knit-ting bag at her feet. They peered in to see what might have been a brown and white ball of yarn.

Bonnie, who was nearest, goggled in disbelief. "That's a *puppy!*"

"A little baby dog," Jamie whispered, down on all fours and creeping forward. The tiny animal stirred and stumbled to his feet. His brown eyes blinked in the light.

Neil crumpled down on his heels and reached out a trembly hand. One finger touched a warm, silky ear to make sure the dog was real. "Oh, thank you, Mrs. Atkins. Thank you." He lifted up the puppy and held him close. His thumb got licked by a little red tongue.

Hattie Atkins' walnut-shell face crinkled down at them. "He's six weeks old come Wednesday. An American beagle hound. My nephew in Salisbury raises them. This one's the best of the lot. Or so he tells me."

"What's his name?" Jamie asked.

Neil didn't even have to think. "Joe-Pye Weed," he said. He knew that was the name of his dog.

"Welcome to your new home, Joe-Pye," Dad said, gently shaking a white front paw.

"He's just what we've been needing," Mother said. "How kind you are, Mrs. Atkins."

"Nonsense," she answered, getting up. "I hope, Neil, you and Joe-Pye will come visit Sarsaparilla and me from time to time."

"We will, all right," Neil promised. "He can ride in the basket on my bike till he grows too big."

Before Hattie Atkins left, Jamie led her into the family room to admire the *Mayflower* on the mantle. "Excellent craftsmanship!" she declared, bobbing her head so positively her earrings danced. "I expect you'll become an architect like your father someday."

"Not me," Neil said emphatically. "I'd rather be a Judo champ. Or do something with animals, like a lion trainer or — well, I'm not exactly sure yet."

"*I'm* going to be an architect," Bonnie announced. "I've been thinking about it a lot lately and that's what I want to be." This was news to the whole family. "Besides, I've got scads of good ideas to make a better school."

"Great girl," Dad said, giving her a warm hug. "I'll have to change my sign to read F. W. Applewhite and Daughter."

Mother and Hattie Atkins exchanged delighted

glances. "No reason in the world she can't carry on the family name," Hattie Atkins said. Jamie, not to be outdone, chipped in, "I'm going to be a policeman. Like Officer Kroznick. I'll give you all a ride in my police car and put the siren on, too."

"Would you like a ride down the road in my car, before I go home?" Hattie Atkins asked him.

"Would I! Oh, please, Mommy, I want to."

They watched Jamie depart with Hattie Atkins as though with a life-long friend. Neil carried Joe-Pye out to the kitchen to give him a bowl of milk while Dad spread newspapers on the floor and Mother found a soft old pillow for his bed. Bonnie let Applesauce in and she circled the newcomer warily.

"I know you're busy," Dad said to Neil. "But when you get a minute, how about taking care of this." He handed him the Judo registration card which he had signed in his blocky black scrawl.

"Yippee! What a day. Don't worry, I'll take care of that, all right! Thanks a heap, Dad. And listen, if you wanta show me how to fix broken windows and repair stuff like that, I'd just as soon learn. But no more models."

"That's a deal."

"I'll order your Judo suit first thing tomorrow morning," Mother said. "You'll have it before the first lesson."

"Wow. I gotta call Fish. Joe-Pye's gone back to sleep. Watch him for me, huh, Bonnie?"

"Sure I will. I'm going to show him to Scott when he comes. It's almost four."

Fish answered the telephone on the first ring. "Got some good news for you," Neil said, tumbling over his words he was talking so fast. "My Dad signed my Judo card — the ink's still wet. Had a lota problems I couldn't explain but none of that matters now. The *Mayflower*'s done and I'm going to get a Judo *gi* like yours. And oh, Fish, you know what?"

"More good news?" Fish asked. Neil could tell by his voice that he was happy inside and that they were friends again.

"The best. I've got a new dog. A beagle six weeks old. Name's Joe-Pye Weed."

"Terrific! I wanta see him. But look, can't you come over and practice that hold? It's no good alone and we haven't even tried out the mats yet."

"Sure can. Be right over. See you, Fish."

"See you, Neil."

Neil got as far as the driveway when he heard a loud "Psst!" It came from the lilac bushes. He turned around and saw Trigger Deal in his red windbreaker, waiting for him.

"What do you want?" Neil asked, barely stopping.

"Slow down, kid. I saw the Atkins' Model T outside your house and I hadda find out if my name came up. She blab to your folks anything about you and me and her bird?"

"Nope."

Trigger eyed him suspiciously. "Ya mean neither of us is in the soup?"

"That's right."

"Hmmmm." Trigger blinked his eyes as he pondered this news. In return, he made up his mind to share some news of his own. "I done you a favor," he announced.

"How come?"

"I wasn't goin' to tell ya, but ya know that ransom money I grabbed from you? It was *marked bills!* I almost jumped outa my skin when I heard it. Would ja believe an old biddy like that was right on the ball! She's somethin' else and I oughta take lessons."

"She's special, all right," Neil agreed.

"S'pose we'll never know how she got her parrot back but she did, she's no loser. As for the ransom, if you'da spent that money, you'd be in jail by now," Trigger said. "That's what I saved you from."

"Oh. Well, thanks."

"Course *I* couldn't keep it, neither. There went my hockey skates, right out the window. Never worked so hard for nothin'." He banged his fist into his palm. "I bet with them I coulda been top man on anybody's team."

"Me, too," Neil said. "You've sure got great muscles."

"You're not bad, kid," Trigger said, giving him a poke on the shoulder. "No hard feelings?"

"No hard feelings." Neil held up his first two fingers. "Peace!" Then he dashed off to Fish's garage to practice Judo with him in their own private gym for the rest of the afternoon.